# Rich Wives Association

# Rich Wives Association

*INDIA*

www.urbanbooks.net

Urban Books, LLC
300 Farmingdale Road, N.Y.-Route 109
Farmingdale, NY 11735

ISBN 13: 978-1-64556-305-1
ISBN 10: 1-64556-305-7

First Trade Paperback Printing April 2022
Printed in the United States of America

10 9 8 7 6 5 4 3 2 1

*This is a work of fiction. Any references or similarities
to actual events, real people, living or dead, or to real
locales are intended to give the novel a sense of reality.
Any similarity in other names, characters, places, and
incidents is entirely coincidental.*

Distributed by Kensington Publishing Corp.
Submit Orders to:
Customer Service
400 Hahn Road
Westminster, MD 21157-4627
Phone: 1-800-733-3000
Fax: 1-800-659-2436

# Rich Wives Association

by

*INDIA*

# Acknowledgments

First and foremost, I must give honor to God for allowing me another opportunity to live my dream. I can't express the feeling I get every time I see my vision complete and brought to life. The cover makes it real, the edit makes it complete, but the readers make it worth it. There is so much gratitude in my heart for each and every one of you. Your support and encouraging words are unyielding and have been from day one. Thank you all from the bottom of my heart.

Without you, no one would know about *The Real Hoodwives of Detroit, Gangstress, Dope, Death, and Deception, Still Deceiving, Detroit City Mafia, Platinum Persuasion, Married to the Money,* and *Rich Wives Association.* Please continue to rock with me, and let's take this thing all the way to the top.

Love Always & Forever,
India

# The Beginning of the End

"911, what's the emergency?" a chipper operator answered the call.

"I would like to report a double homicide."

"Excuse me, but did you say you're calling to report a double homicide?" the operator asked.

"Yes! Two people are dead," I said calmly.

"What's your location?"

"I'm at the Dell Hotel in room 616," I answered.

"Okay, stay calm. Police and emergency medical units have been dispatched. Help is on the way." The operator sounded alarmed. "Are you in any danger?"

"No. Not anymore," I replied, feeling the safest I'd felt in a very long time.

"Is the assailant still on the premises? Is he or she nearby?"

"Yes, she's here. As a matter of fact, she's so close I can touch her," I said while placing the palm of my hand against the mirror.

"I'm going to stay on the phone with you until help arrives," the operator conveyed.

"Help better get here fast before there's one more body added to the number." Dropping the phone into the sink, I placed the gun to my head, prepared to take what was left of my existence.

It seemed like just yesterday when I was popping bottles and tags without a care in the world. Today, here I was contemplating suicide. I had everything, or at least

I thought I did, until reality showed me that fame didn't come easy. The life of a celebrity wife is supposed to be all glitz and glamour. With red carpets, black cards, and tons of green money, who wouldn't want to be on the A-list? However, when the lights dim and the paparazzi fade, living life in the fab lane comes with a price. Some of us pay severely for our membership in the Rich Wives Association. Don't believe? Here's our story.

# Chapter One

## *Jasmine*

"Pregnant! Are you sure?" I damn near screamed at Dr. Shiloh, my gynecologist.

"Jasmine, let's not act too surprised by this news." She rolled her eyes and wagged her finger in my face. "Come on now. We've been down this road too many times for you to be stunned." Dr. Shiloh was from India. Her English was excellent, but her native tongue was still present and particularly noticeable.

"How did I let this happen?" I said more to myself than her. I was sure she knew I wasn't speaking to her, but that didn't stop her from chiming in anyway.

"Jasmine, they make condoms and birth control for a reason, you know."

Now Dr. Shiloh was my girl and all, but she was beginning to piss me off. She had been my doctor ever since I was 17. She even delivered my son, Jordan. However, with the way I was feeling right now, if she kept talking, I was going to have to get ugly with her. This was not the time for speeches and "I told you so's." Right now, all I needed was a damn hug!

"Dr. Shiloh, please not right now, okay?" I wiped at a tear that slipped down the side of my face. I was so disappointed in myself I didn't know what to do. This was my fifth pregnancy and would end up being my fourth abortion. Before you smack your lips and begin to judge me for what I'd done, you should try asking me what my story is and where my pain comes from.

Life for me might have appeared to be glamorous to blog writers, magazine readers, and television viewers. But trust and believe, life for me was no walk in the park by most people's standards. My name was Jasmine James. I was 26 years old and married to the hip-hop legend King James. No, not LeBron, the basketball player from Ohio. My man was King James, the super-hot lyrical genius from the west side of Detroit.

Although King was his birth name, he went by KJ for obvious reasons. He was a six-foot, two-inch brother with light skin, beautiful teeth, wavy hair, and swag to die for. On a scale of one to ten, baby was at least an eleven. He got his break and was discovered about four years ago by Byron Washington, the CEO of Independent Records. After the contract was signed, King finally achieved fame, and our lives changed instantly. Most people pray for shit like this. However, if I was being honest, this celebrity life was for the birds.

I longed for the old days when we shared a studio apartment, rode the bus, and ate McDonald's every day. Crazy, right? Well, it was true. Money had changed KJ in the worst way. In some ways, I was afraid it changed me too. No, I wouldn't have said I was stuck up or anything like that. I still shopped in the hood at the local malls, and I could still chill in the cut and kick it with my people. But my standards had been lowered. Lately, my tolerance for King's bullshit was extremely high, and that wasn't okay with me. I'd watched him turn into my beautiful nightmare. I needed to wake up, open my eyes, and walk away, but I couldn't. I just couldn't.

See, I'd loved King since we were in kindergarten. During recess one day, he asked me to be his woman and gave me a dollar and a kiss on the cheek. I cried, took the dollar, and told the teacher. King got a timeout, but he won my heart that day and had held it ever since. We were inseparable! He was my man, and I was his bitch! Ride or die, I was by his side. After high school, he did some time upstate on a weapons charge. My mama wasn't feeling him, but I had his back. I stuck out the three-year bid with him, and when he was released, I was standing at the front gate, arms wide open. It was then that he informed me that his new passion was rapping. I encouraged him to take action and pursue a rap career. Within months, his music ripped through Detroit like a virus. Eventually, other states began to take notice. Just like that, he was signed. Life couldn't have gotten any better. Or so we thought.

We soon discovered that I was pregnant, and I was given the news that we would be having a boy. King was the happiest man in the world. He wanted everything to be perfect for our son. He got down on one knee and asked me to marry him right here in Dr. Shiloh's office. Of course, my answer was yes. Hence, we were married two months later. The lavish wedding, the exotic honeymoon, and purchasing our first mega-home was a breeze and no sweat off our backs. King had been signed for approximately six months by then. Money was flowing and everything was velvet. Actually, it was up until the night my water broke and Jordan was born.

Labor for me was extremely difficult. I felt as if I were dying. In my heart, I knew something was wrong. After Jordan was cleaned up and in my arms, I counted his ten tiny fingers and toes. I peered into his beautiful brown eyes and inspected his little ears, too. Everything was present and accounted for, but something was off. Staring at my son, it was then that I noticed he looked a little different from most babies and his cry wasn't normal.

Nobody said a word to me, not even King, my mother, or Dr. Shiloh. They all noticed it too but were afraid to say it aloud. The next day, Jordan was taken for a hearing test and his circumcision. About three hours later, he was returned to me with both good and bad news. The good news was he didn't have any hearing problems. The bad news was he had been diagnosed with Down syndrome.

After receiving that information, I was a mess. I blamed myself and cried constantly for my son. I was devastated that in less than twenty-four hours after coming into the world, he already had odds against him. King was crushed. Instantly, I began to feel a disconnection between us. Although he didn't admit it initially, he blamed me for Jordan's disorder, and that shit hurt like hell. How can you get through one of the most difficult situations in your life when the person holding your hand lets go?

He began to stay out late and party a little more. Within months, King was all over the internet. He was rumored to have been with this model or that singer and even a few groupies. There was also mention of a few outside children, which as of yet hadn't been confirmed. I never questioned him about the stories that I heard or read. Honestly, I didn't want to know the answer. All that mattered to me was that he provided for me and Jordan. It didn't matter that the rumors were probably true, because deep down, I knew he loved us. This was just his way of dealing with things. I didn't doubt his love at all. However, it did hurt my feelings that he rarely wanted to have sex when he came home from his tours.

On the rare occasions when we did get it on, he always used condoms. Fearing the worst, like an STD or something, I asked him what the deal was. He admitted that he didn't want any more children. His rationale was because he was working all the time. Therefore, he didn't want me to have to handle two kids all by myself. I assured him that it didn't matter to me, that I would love to try again.

Aside from caring for Jordan and the occasional shopping trip, I wasn't doing much with my time anyway. He still refused. I was aware that it was because he didn't want another child like Jordan. I understood that most people couldn't deal with having a special-needs child, so I backed off. We went back to using condoms. After one broke, I was told that I was once again expecting. King hit the roof and made me get an abortion. I didn't want to do it, but my hands were tied. The same thing took place with the second unplanned pregnancy, as well as the third.

Every time I had to get on top of that table and kill a piece of me, I slipped further and further into a deep, dark hole. I begged Dr. Shiloh to tie my tubes, but she refused. "You're young! One day you will meet a man who wants to make beautiful babies with you, and you will be sorry," she had said.

"Dr. Shiloh, I'm already married to King, and he ain't going nowhere." I had flashed her my rock as if she could ever forget him.

"He is no good for you, and he is damaging your insides." She had scribbled something down on a prescription pad. "Take this to the pharmacy, and I don't want to see you back here until your annual pap smear." She handed me the paper, which was a prescription for birth control. "No more babies, Jasmine." Those were her famous last words.

That was four months ago. I was mortified to be sitting in her office with the same problem for the fourth time.

"Jasmine, you are too smart to be so naive. Please, honey, at least keep this baby! This may be your last chance at a normal pregnancy," she pleaded as I nodded.

I wasn't saying I was going to keep the baby, but I did agree that this just might be my last opportunity. It would be wonderful to have another baby and prove to

King that we could do it right. Unfortunately, I knew he wouldn't be a happy camper.

"Jasmine, here are a few samples of prenatal vitamins. If you decide to keep this one, start taking them as soon as possible."

# Chapter Two

## *Tionne*

I looked around the 30,000-square-foot California mansion in disgust. No longer could I see the beauty within this gated property. Gone was the love I once had for the home and its co-owner, my husband. Every painting on the wall and expensive piece of furniture was just another reminder of his bullshit.

"Tionne, where the fuck are you going?" Dallas looked over the marble banister. He was standing there in a pair of black silk pajama bottoms. The oil on his chocolate brown skin was illuminated by the scented candles lined along the ledge. Every muscle in his chest and stomach area stuck out like a sore thumb. Dallas was a powerhouse! Had my husband not been one of the most famous rappers turned CEO of his own music label, he could definitely be mistaken for a professional bodybuilder.

"I'm leaving." I kneeled down to pick up the two pieces of Louis Vuitton luggage resting near my Giuseppe-covered feet.

"You ain't going nowhere, especially with only two suitcases." Dallas chuckled.

I even giggled a bit too. With all the clothing, shoes, and other worldly possessions upstairs in my closet, it did seem quite ridiculous to only be leaving with a few items. Even so, I decided long ago that if and when the time came to leave, I would only leave with whatever I'd come with. It was time for me to make my own way in life. I didn't want Dallas to take credit for anything, not even the labels across my round ass.

"Come on, baby. Join me in bed and stop playing."

"Dallas, I'm serious." I had threatened more than two dozen times to leave his no-good, two-timing ass. Each time I meant it but could never stay true to my word. It seemed as if he had an invisible hold on me. No one could see it, but everyone knew it was there.

"Look, I'm not about to stand here all night. Quit playing, and bring your sexy ass to bed." Dallas made his way down the semi-spiral staircase, taking each stair at a deliberately slow pace.

I didn't have time for this nonsense tonight. He thought my threats were idle, but he was gon' learn today.

"You got another nigga or something?" Dallas teased me with a laugh.

He knew I would always be his, and so did I, or so I once thought. "I should have another two or three. Hell, maybe four or five just to keep up with you," I said with my back to him.

"Ten niggas couldn't even love you like I do," Dallas barked.

I could hear the flopping sound of his leather house shoes nearing. Without delay, my entire body tensed up. Every time I was prepared to walk away from him and his lies, he always found his way back in. The majority of the time, Dallas would apologize profusely for his behavior. Then he tried to make things better with a new piece of jewelry, an expensive new car, or a shopping spree. Sadly, he only got his act together long enough for me to let my guard down. Just when I thought my marriage would be okay, his ass would end up in the doghouse again.

"Baby girl, did you hear me?" Dallas reached down to remove a piece of luggage from my tight grip. "I said I'm sorry. I love you."

"Dallas, you don't love nothing but pussy." I rolled my catlike eyes, which were a mixture of hazel and gray contacts of course.

"I can't argue with that." Dallas stroked his neatly trimmed goatee, then rubbed a hand across his bald head. "If I didn't love pussy, I'd be gay."

"You know what I mean." I smacked my full lips. The MAC lip paint shimmered beneath the lights of the chandelier hanging in the foyer.

"Can't we talk about it?" His brown eyes peered into mine.

"Talk about what, Dallas? This is ho number fifteen!" I snapped. Normally, I was a quiet person until you pissed me off. "If you want to talk about why that bitch was under your desk sucking your dick when I came to the office, then go ahead. Be my guest." Truthfully, she wasn't even the real reason I was leaving. I was simply fed up with him, period. I was tired of the way his forehead wrinkled when he smiled. I was tired of the way he left toothpaste all over the sink. I was tired of the way he slept at night, and I was tired of him always leaving the toilet seat up. More than anything, I was tired of taking chances with my life every time I slept with him. It was time that I had some much-needed space. Catching him with this new bitch made leaving that much easier.

"I told you she was down there shining my shoes," he lied to me with a straight face.

"Oh, she was polishing something all right, but it damn sure wasn't your shoes." I shook my head. Dallas was pathetic. His lies weren't even good anymore.

"You're jumping to conclusions. From your position at the door, it may have looked like my joint was in her mouth, but it wasn't. I swear!" He raised his right hand as if he were taking an oath.

"Dallas, just shut the fuck up! There's nothing you can say or do that will persuade me to change my mind. I'm leaving and that's that."

"I thought you were in this shit for better or worse. Until death do we part, remember?" He tossed the wedding vows at me like they mattered.

I had already endured the good, the bad, the ugly, and the most horrific shit imaginable. There were no more burdens for me to bear in this marriage. I was done!

"Dallas, don't bring up our vows. You and I both know they don't mean shit to you." Sighing from irritation, I stretched my neck to look past my husband. Through the stained glass surrounding our front door, I could see that it was raining cats and dogs outside. It made me reminisce about our wedding day many years ago.

*The day was June 21, 2001, a Saturday afternoon at Hebron Sinai Baptist Church in Detroit, Michigan, and despite the protests of upcoming rapper Black Bishop, aka Dallas Foster, family and friends gathered inside the medium-sized church for our humble ceremony. He had been in the music industry for about two years and felt that our wedding should be a top-notch event rather than some average shit. I, on the other hand, wasn't for the glitz and glamour. I wanted my wedding to be eloquent yet modest, just as I was. See, I was just an old-fashioned girl in love with being in love. Many of my girlfriends thought I had hit the jackpot when Dallas proposed. He wasn't the cutest man on earth initially, but wealth had made the nigga finer over the years. They thought I only said yes for a paycheck, but I swear on a stack of bibles that money had nothing to do with it.*

*"Well, my dear, there's been a change of plans," Niles, my wedding planner announced as he entered the pastor's office. On this day, the small white room was serving as a makeshift dressing room for me. My dress hung on the back of the door, my shoes rested on the brown leather sofa, and I sat in the pastor's chair, getting my makeup done.*

*"What now?" I asked with sarcasm in my voice. There had already been more catastrophes that morning than I wanted to count. First, my dress didn't fit, and the flowers were wrong. Next, the ring bearer had gotten sick, throwing up all over his suit, and finally, one of my bridesmaids was stuck in Florida after a layover flight.*

*"Honey, there is a severe thunderstorm headed this way. I even heard mention of a tornado. I'm afraid the outside reception won't happen today, my love." Niles rubbed my back, instinctively trying to soften the blow. "I hate to stress my brides before their wedding about things I can fix. Regrettably though, there's nothing I can do about Mother Nature."*

*"A tornado!" I shouted along with my mother and the makeup artist.*

*"Detroit doesn't have tornadoes!" Unwilling to accept what he was telling me, I shook my head vigorously, causing the makeup artist to momentarily stop drawing on my face.*

*"There will be one today, love." Niles unbuttoned his suit coat and kneeled down beside me. "Police have asked everyone to remain where they are until this thing blows over."*

*"What does that mean?" asked Toni, my mother.*

*"No one can leave here, and more than likely, no one else will show up," Niles continued.*

*"Baby, maybe we should do this on another day," Toni said reluctantly. "I know how important today is for you, baby girl, but—"*

*"Mama, I know you have reservations about this marriage, but this tornado can't last forever. We'll just have to wait, because I am getting married today," I replied on the brink of tears. I loved Dallas with every fiber in my being. He was my high school sweetheart, my first love, and my first sexual partner. Nothing would ruin my nuptials, not even some punk-ass tornado.*

*"Okay, baby, we'll give you a little time to think about it," my mother added like she hadn't just heard me say I was still getting married.*

*"Whatever," I snapped. My mother was really working my nerves today, and I wanted to tell her a thing or two or five, but I exhaled and closed my eyes. Silently, everyone left me in the office alone with my thoughts.*

*It'd been two hours of unsuccessfully waiting for the storm to pass, and there was a knock at the door. It was my mother again. "Hey, pumpkin, are you feeling better?" She closed the door and approached me where*

*I was now sitting on the pastor's leather sofa. I was wrapped in a robe with rollers in my hair and a full face of makeup, just staring through the picture window behind the pastor's desk. From my seat, I could see how dark it was outside. The trees were swaying from side to side, and I could hear the wind howling violently. Mrs. Bernie, the church secretary, was running around outside trying to chase the huge hat that had just flown off her head. I wanted to laugh, but my mood was somber.*

*"This is the worst day ever! Why is God letting this happen to me?" I turned my attention away from the window to face my mother, who was frowning. I realized my question was upsetting to my mother. Toni had raised me to never question the works of God.*

*"Baby, I believe God is trying to get your attention." She took a seat beside me, then cradled me in her arms. "Maybe this is a sign that you and Dallas shouldn't be joined in matrimony."*

I remembered being so angry back then, wanting to curse my mother out, but oh, how true her words were. I wished I could tell Toni she was right. Sadly, she succumbed to breast cancer three years ago. My one and only rock was gone.

"What is wrong with you?" Dallas waved his hand in front of my face. "Have you been listening to me at all?"

"Look, I'm leaving. This time I won't let you stop me." I snatched my luggage back from him.

"Where are you going? There's nowhere better than this." He raised his arms in a God-like manner to indicate all the things I would be leaving behind. Dallas was a man of means. He knew most bitches would kill for the lifestyle he provided me. I was sure he thought I was a fool to leave it all behind. "You have a twenty-four-hour chef, a maid who cleans for you, and private yachts and jets at your disposal, yet you're leaving?"

"That don't mean shit if you can't be faithful!" I spat. "I'm sick of you and your hoes, Dallas. I can do better by myself, and I will." As I made my way to the large door, Dallas couldn't prevent himself from tossing one more insult my way.

"Bitch, I made you," he screamed. "I made your ass, Tionne, from the teeth in your fucking mouth to those shoes on your goddamn feet!"

I stopped dead in my tracks at his startling revelation. Dallas had insulted me before but never on this level. When I was a child, my mother used to tell me that words would never hurt. On the contrary, that comment felt like an ass whooping for real. What hurt even more than his words was the fact that he was right.

A natural beauty, I possessed brown skin, a few freckles, and sandy red hair. My body was well proportioned with perfect D-cups, a medium waist, and an especially round ass. Sadly, once Dallas made it into the industry, I was no longer good enough. He turned me into what society considered to be pretty. My gapped teeth were covered with Lumineers. My freckles were concealed with makeup. My beautiful hair was dyed coal black, then stuffed with heavy extensions. Dallas also gifted me with a personal trainer. Although my frame was already nice, in a matter of months, I was sculpted into a stone-cold masterpiece.

Turning to look at Dallas, I smiled like a madwoman. "You're right, D. You do own the shoes on my feet." I slipped off the black spiked wedges. "You also own the jeans on my ass," I said. I slid out of the spandex Jessica Red jeans, then tossed them at my husband. "I probably purchased this T-shirt with your money, so it also belongs to you." As I removed the top, Dallas reached for his dick. I was sure my little striptease was right up his alley. The Victoria's Secret bra and panties appeared to be painted on my body. He was turned on, I was sure. Next, I removed the bob-cut black lace-front weave and tossed it to the floor. "Last but not least, you can have this, too!" I was done living life according to Dallas.

"What are you doing?" he asked, no longer aroused but annoyed.

"I'm leaving!" I grabbed my luggage and chucked him the fucking deuces.

# Chapter Three

## *Zuri Monae*

As soon as the polar white 2015 Mercedes-Benz C 300 with almond interior and chrome exterior pulled up to the stairs of the grand Victorian mansion, my stomach cringed. Without a word, I watched as Sturgis, our chauffeur, put the vehicle in park before stepping out to open our doors. Part of me wanted to grasp my door handle and hang on for dear life. However, it would've only delayed the inevitable.

"Have a nice evening, Mrs. Armstrong." Sturgis looked almost apologetic for not prolonging the ride home from the preliminary boxing match that my husband had just lost. "I'll be here at six a.m. sharp, Mr. Armstrong." Sturgis nodded at my husband before jumping back inside the whip and pulling off like a stunt driver in an action movie. Because I knew what was about to happen, my heart raced and panic set in.

"Come on, sweetheart." Jason, aka One-Two Armstrong, reached for my hand to assist me up the stairs. Standing at six feet, my husband was stunning with perfect chocolate skin, ultra-white teeth, and a deep dimple in his chin. Additionally, he was charismatic and could charm the panties off anyone with a vagina. To the world, I had done well for myself by locking him down. Conversely, only Jason and I knew the monster he could become given the right situation or circumstance.

With a smile, yet trembling, I placed my hand into his and ascended the stairs. The silence was deadly as we walked up thirteen cobblestone steps toward the front door. I counted each one to take my mind off the misery yet to come.

Upon entrance into the quiet home we shared with our infant daughter, I watched as Jason removed his Armani suit jacket and then his big-face Oyster 48 mm rose gold Rolex covered in diamonds. Casually, he laid the piece of expensive jewelry I'd given him after a big win last year on the foyer table, then tossed his jacket atop it.

"Baby, you did really well tonight. Those judges were stu—"

I never got the chance to complete the sentence before Jason balled up his massive fist and punched me right in the stomach. Naturally, I doubled over in pain. That was when he came with an uppercut to my chin, sending me stumbling backward.

"Stop it! Jason, stop it please!" I screamed for all of California to hear me. No matter how many times this occurred, I never could get used to the pain.

Wrapping his hand around my throat, Jason lifted my almost-anorexic frame off the floor. Although I stood nearly six feet tall, only the tips of my toes could touch the cherry-oak floor.

"Please," I begged, but Jason was in a zone. Anytime he lost a preliminary fight or experienced any type of disappointment in life, he sent blows and body shots my way. Although his hands were registered in all fifty states as lethal weapons, he continuously used me as a punching bag because he knew I would take it and wouldn't dare call the police. Why would I? Calling the police on him meant tarnishing his reputation. A tarnished reputation didn't put food on the table. Ultimately, it took money out of my household. Yeah, I know you're over there in disbelief at what I said, but I'm just keeping it one hundred.

As a 35-year-old five-division world champion, the 1996 silver medal winner of the Olympics, and undefeated heavyweight boxer in his class, my husband was worth well over $900 million. He was a big deal with several endorsements as well as his own sports representation agency. The life that Jason provided me outweighed his temper tantrums.

"Stop that shit right damn now!" Sylvia, Jason's mother, yelled from the top of the stairs. She was peering over the railing with a disapproving look. "Jason Renaldo Armstrong, what in the hell has gotten into you?"

"I lost my preliminary match." Jason stopped battering my body, then turned toward his mother. I tried to pull myself together. However, my bearings were off due to the lack of oxygen.

"Lost what? Your goddamn mind, that's what." Sylvia flew down the steps to assist me. "Zuri, do you want me to call for help?"

"No," I screamed. "No police. I'll be fine." I nodded before collecting the Alexander McQueens that had come off my feet during the beatdown.

"She'll be fine, Mama." Jason briefly glanced at me before climbing the stairs dismissively. That was his ritual. He would beat the snot out of me, then lock himself in the bedroom so he wouldn't have to see what he'd done.

"Is Jelly asleep?" That's what we called my daughter Angelica.

"Been asleep for hours." Sylvia stood in the middle of the foyer with both hands on her hips, looking puzzled. "Why are you acting like you just didn't take an ass whooping from a professional boxer?" Sylvia lived in New York. Therefore, she had never borne witness to her son's rage. Currently, she was in town to visit for a month to help care for Jelly. I was thankful she was here to stop the violence, especially tonight.

"This ain't nothing new. Just leave it alone, Syl." Although the right side of my face was lumped up, I tried as best I could to smile.

She grabbed my arm and whispered, "How long he been beating on you?"

I started not to reply because it was none of her business, but I knew my mother-in-law wouldn't let it go, so I gave in. "You remember his twenty-sixth birthday party? The one you threw him in Hawaii and invited everybody to?" I looked on as she recalled the event.

"Yeah. That's when his punk-ass daddy 'missed' the flight and didn't make it." Sylvia made air quotes with a frown. "Jason was so angry."

"That's when it started."

"That was nine years ago, Zuri. Why haven't you put an end to this? I know that's my son, but his ass needs to be dealt with for putting his hands on you. You need to call the police," Sylvia urged.

"I can't call the police on him, Syl. Jason and Jelly are all I have in this world." With those words, I limped up the stairs.

"Zuri Monae," Sylvia called out in a mother-like yet scolding manner. I turned to face her. "Look at you. You're a stunning supermodel with your own awards and accolades. Baby, you have to learn to love yourself more than you love my son."

Sylvia thought she was dropping knowledge on me. However, I wanted to tell her that love had nothing to do with it. Money meant power, and cash was king in my world.

Born and bred in the slums of Kingston, Jamaica, I had endured far worse for much less. I'd overcome being beaten by my grandmother, raped by my uncle, and abandoned by both of my parents. Yep, that's right. My father, Nada, and my mother, Bambi, left your girl when I was only 2 years old to head for the United States. Their intentions were to secure work and living quarters, then send for me. But you know how the story goes. They got caught up in the ways of the world and never looked back.

Day in and day out, I would watch the mail with hopes of a letter from the U.S. After several years of waiting, I learned that I was all I had. I made a vow that, no matter what, I would leave the slums and head for higher ground. True to my word, at the age of 22, I used my silky skin and long legs to catwalk out of the ghetto. America had been good to me, but Jason had been even better. Life was great aside from his periodic bullshit. At least now I had tissue dipped in 24-karat gold to catch my tears, which was more than I could say for other women in my situation.

# Chapter Four

## *Diamond*

The buzzing sound disrupted my slumber. Turning on my side, I grabbed the iPhone and answered, "Hello."

"Happy b-day, sis," Dexter, my older brother, yelled into the speaker.

"Thanks, bro." I turned the volume on my phone down to drown out the noise in his background. It sounded as if he was at a party.

"Girl, it's early. I know you ain't asleep."

"Yeah, I was. I had a long day," I yawned.

"Doing what? Shopping and spending money?" He laughed.

"No, nigga. I was working," I snapped.

"I'm sorry. I didn't know conning men out of their money was such a strenuous occupation," he retorted.

"The fuck you mean?" I cut into him for trying to ho me.

"Look, I didn't call to start no shit. I was only calling to wish you a happy birthday."

"I'll call you tomorrow. Be safe out there," I said before ending the call and dropping the phone. Although I wanted to be pissed off with my brother, how could I? He was right. Not long ago, conning men and running scams was my full-time job, and I was good at what I did. You can think what you want, but a bitch had to eat. This poor girl from the projects managed to hustle her way up to penthouses and Porsche cars.

You see, after administering all the game I could on the male residents of St. Louis, I packed my shit and headed to Hollywood. I knew the money was in Tinseltown, and I was bound to eventually snag an actor or a Beverly Hills surgeon. I landed a job at an exclusive exotic dance club in Melrose and immersed myself in the "in" crowd. Before long, I was going on dates with musicians, producers, and the like. It felt good to be arm candy until I realized it was time to secure a future. I no longer wanted to be a fling, weekend thing, or a jump off. It was time to become a wife. Unfortunately, I didn't have any prospects until a chance encounter with my new boo, Kensington Tucker, who was the starting shooting guard for the Los Angeles Lakers.

The night we met in Los Angeles at a twenty-four-hour diner on La Cienega Boulevard was purely coincidental. I'd gone there to pick up a steak and lobster meal after leaving the strip club, and he was dining with an entourage. The place was packed. Therefore, I had to stand in line for nearly thirty minutes waiting for a table before I was finally granted access into the diner. Upon entering, I spotted the famous NBA star at the table shooting the breeze with his squad. He was larger than life and finer than I recalled him being on television.

Without a word, I made my way past his table, then sat down in my booth. From my position, I could hear all the chatter among him and his friends. His smile was captivating and his laugh adorable. I remembered seeing an interview with him during playoffs. He seemed to be very humble and kind. You didn't find that these days with professional athletes. Because of that, someway, somehow, I had to make my mark on Ken. Regrettably, from my position, I could also see several obstacles in my way. They were called groupie bitches. Several of them surrounded the table of men, practically falling over themselves to get an autograph or a picture. Some of them were cuter than me and slimmer than my size eight.

Nonetheless, I one-upped the competition by calling Ken's waitress.

"Oh, I'm sorry. I'm not the waitress for this section. She's on her way though," she had said.

"I would like to pay his bill." I had pointed to the tableful of food and beverages.

"There are twelve people on his tab. Are you sure?" She had frowned. "His bill is almost one thousand dollars."

"I got it." Without worry, I'd reached inside my Birkin bag, then placed ten big-face Franklins in her hand.

"I'll let them know." Bewildered by my actions, she'd stepped away. As I placed my order with my own waitress, I watched as Ken's waitress delivered the news. Every man at the table strained their eyes to see who had just dropped a grand on their meal. When Ken's eyes met mine, I'd simply nodded. I realized my move was bold, but it paid off.

Within minutes, Ken had made it his business to introduce himself to me. The two of us chilled for over an hour. By the end of the night, Ken walked away with admiration and appreciation for an independent woman such as myself, and I walked away with his digits. We chatted every day thereafter, and within three months, he asked me to be his girl. That was six months ago. Since then, I'd been trying to stay on the straight and narrow. I had it good with Ken, and I planned to rock with him until the wheels fell off.

"Happy birthday to you
    Happy birthday to you
    Happy birthday, dear Diamond, soon-to-be Mrs. Tucker
    Happy birthday to you"

Speaking of Ken, he barged into the bedroom, singing and wearing nothing except an apron, a pair of Jordans, boxers, and a chef's hat. He was carrying something covered by a bronze lid on a tray with fancy silverware, a linen napkin, and a small vase with a red rose.

"Aww, snap! Don't tell me you been down there cooking for a sista?" I sat up in the twelve-foot circular custom bed and hit the light on the nightstand.

"I'll do anything for my baby, especially on her birthday." Ken displayed the contagious smile that made me fall for him all over again.

"Thank you, baby, but what is it?" I looked over at the tray cautiously. I had never known Ken to cook anything, so I was a little scared.

"Girl, this here is the joint." He lifted the lid, and steam hit me in the face. When the smoke cleared, I was in awe of the culinary masterpiece before me.

"Baby, you did not bake this chicken, candy these yams, or cook this macaroni." I shook my head.

"I did too, and I got the dishes downstairs to prove it." Ken sat his lanky six-foot-seven frame down on the bed beside me. "I had to call in the big guns to pull this off."

"You called your mother?" I replied, already knowing who the big gun was.

"Yeah, I Skyped her, and she talked me through the whole thing," Ken admitted. "She said she has to meet the woman who has me in the kitchen because she must be special."

"Is that right?" I grabbed the gold fork and dug into my food.

"I told her we'll set up something soon with the whole family."

"You must be feeling your girl if you're trying to take me home." I smiled at my man. Although he was 26 and covered in tattoos with tons of facial hair, Ken possessed a baby face and boyish good looks.

"Hell yeah, I'm feeling you. If I weren't, you wouldn't be here." With a chuckle, Ken stood from the bed.

"Where are you going?"

"I have to clean up the kitchen."

"Let the maid do it, bae," I whined. He was only in town for a few more days until he returned to Denver for training camp. Consequently, I wanted to spend every minute with him.

"She doesn't come back until tomorrow. Besides, your nigga is a neat freak." Ken was right. In his condo, everything had a place. His walk-in closet was organized to a T. All of his clothes were categorized with areas for sportswear, casual wear, and special events. All 400 pairs of his shoes were in plastic containers with a picture on the front so he would know what was in each box without removing the lid. Even his jewelry section looked like the display counter at Diamonds International.

"On my way downstairs, I'll run you a bath," Ken called out before entering the bathroom in the guest suite that I slept in.

"Will you come back up and join me?" I asked seductively.

"You know I can't, Diamond." Ken was super religious with regard to abstaining from sex before marriage. He told me he believed his faithfulness to God's Word was what allowed him to be blessed in his NBA career. The brother was super successful and hella paid, so I couldn't argue with his theory. It was, however, hard to play my position. I'm not going to lie. A bitch had needs. Many nights, I contemplated stepping out. Then again, I knew I couldn't afford to lose Ken on account of some random dick, so I played it cool. Furthermore, I had a feeling my ring was coming real soon. Until then, I would continue playing the "good girl" Ken thought I was.

# Chapter Five

## *Lyric*

"Mom, my teacher said you haven't paid my tuition yet, so I can't go on the field trip tomorrow," Leslie, my 12-year-old daughter, said after joining me in the kitchen.

With my eyes wide, I continued scanning the contents of the refrigerator as an attempt to conceal my facial expression from my child. "I was thinking about doing some fish and shrimp tacos for dinner. What do you think, baby?" I asked nonchalantly.

"Mom, did you hear what I said?" Leslie took a seat atop the barstool resting in front of the counter. "My teacher said you haven't paid my tu—"

"I heard you." I closed the sub-zero stainless steel refrigerator doors, then turned to look at my daughter. "Some things came up, baby, and Mommy had to push some bills around. I promise I'll pay it next week."

"Okay." Leslie sighed.

"Where is the field trip going to be?" I knew my daughter was disappointed. Leslie was a good kid who barely asked for anything. I felt like shit to not be able to send her on this trip.

"We were going to the California Science Center." Leslie was a scientist in the making. She loved everything about chemistry, biology, and formulas. This meant she was heartbroken to not be going to the one place she had her heart set on all year. "It's okay. Maybe you and Dad can take me this summer." With a shrug, Leslie turned to leave the kitchen.

"Hold up, baby. Grab the checkbook out of my purse."

"Thank you, Mommy. You're the best!" Leslie flew to retrieve the checkbook and was back in no time. I really couldn't afford the $12,000 for school tuition right at this moment, but it didn't stop me from writing the check like it was nothing. *By the time they cash this, I should have money in the bank.* Writing a bad check was a daring move that could've landed my ass in jail, but dammit, my baby deserved to see the fucking science center.

"Go put that in your book bag, then finish that homework." With a smile, I watched my daughter skip happily away. It felt good to be able to save the day, but I also felt terrible for committing fraud. "The storm won't last forever," I mumbled before returning to the task of making dinner.

"Hello," I said after grabbing the phone from its wall-mounted cradle in the large chef's kitchen with bronze and brown backsplash and matching butcher block countertops.

"Care to comment on your husband's drug habit, Lyric?" a voice heckled on the other end.

"Don't call my house again." Flustered, I ended the call.

"Who was that, bae?" Damien, my husband of eleven years, called from the dining room. He was sitting there reading a script his agent sent by courier this morning.

"Nobody," I lied while holding back tears.

"Well, why are you crying?" Damien entered the kitchen wearing nothing except a pair of Hanes pajama bottoms and a smile. His golden dreadlocks hung over his shoulders, and his hazel eyes sparkled in the light.

"Those tabloid people keep calling the fucking house, and it's pissing me off." I had already changed our number five times. It was supposed to be unlisted, but somehow those fuckers just kept on calling. "I'm tired of this, Damien," I confessed.

"I know, baby. I promise it will get better soon." Damien pulled me into his embrace and held me, allowing my tears to wet his chest.

"When, Damien?" I shouted. My ass was furious. "The fucking bills are past due. The bank is trying to take our house. Hell, we can barely afford food. So tell me when it's going to get better."

"Screaming isn't going to make the situation better." Damien tried to remain calm. He understood that I was hurting and it was all because of him, but I guessed he didn't want the kids to be alarmed. "We'll figure this out."

"I'm tired, Damien. I don't have anything left." I was done with being the resolution expert for everybody in my damn life. The pressure was unreal. Sometimes I just wanted to go to sleep and not wake up, but I knew my children depended on me. "I didn't create this mess. You did. So you fix it." Pulling back, I wiped my eyes and walked away.

As Damien watched silently, I knew he wished he could go back to when life was simple, when we were just two poor kids growing up in Boston. Money and fame had complicated things to no end. Life had taken a turn for the worse. Damien recognized that I was at my breaking point, praying for a breakthrough before it was too late.

Slipping into the guest bathroom on the main floor, I flopped down on the toilet and cried hysterically. I turned on the water to mask my sobbing. Apparently, it didn't work, because within ten minutes, there was a knock on the door.

"Mom, are you all right in there?" Jonah, my 8-year-old son, asked.

"I'm fine, baby. I burned my hand, that's all," I lied.

"Want me to get you some ice?" Jonah called out.

"No, I'll be all right, baby. Just give me a minute, okay?"

"Okay. I love you. I hope you feel better." Jonah was a sweetheart by nature.

"I love you too," I said while suppressing the sound of my cries. However, now the tears flowed quicker than ever. I loved my children with everything I had, but sometimes I wanted to give up. My shoulders had been carrying a heavy load for quite some time, and I was beginning to feel defeated. "Where did we go wrong?" I asked the question aloud, although I already knew the answer.

Eight years ago, Damien and I were on cloud nine. His first sitcom had just been picked up for national syndication. He had also landed a movie role with some of Hollywood's vets. From there, his career took off. Before either of us knew it, we were chartering private jets around the world. Our money flow appeared to be never-ending, and struggling was a thing of the past, until addiction showed up and showed out.

Four years into living the good life, Damien felt the pressure to experiment with some Hollywood friends and cocaine. Soon enough, he was addicted. At first, I paid his habit no mind. Hell, I was too busy enjoying my newfound fame and fortune to pay attention. Being young and naive, I had even dabbled in it a few times with him. Thank God I didn't form an addiction, but the same could not be said for Damien. Initially, I thought my husband was only going through a phase. However, I soon learned otherwise.

After a few run-ins with police and several tantrums on movie sets, Damien found his way into the unemployment line. No one wanted to do business with him. As a result, our bank accounts took a nosedive. Nonetheless, in spite of his downfalls and shortcomings, I remained by his side. I started a celebrity styling business to keep funds coming in. With my connections in the industry, the company took off and was doing numbers. Things were looking up for my family until one of Damien's last bouts with drugs.

As a result, I ended up spending a great deal of money on Damien's treatment as well as bribing the media to keep it hush-hush. I realized it was a gamble when I invested in his sobriety. Even so, it was a risk I was willing to take to save my husband. Unfortunately, the gamble didn't pay off. Damien couldn't even stay clean for six months. For that reason, all of our accounts were in the red. My company was practically bankrupt. Eventually, everyone would know my business—family, friends, and the world. I wasn't ready to face the music and prayed like hell I didn't have to.

Again, someone was pounding on the door. "Jonah, Mommy is fine." I turned the water off and stood.

"It's me, Lyric," Damien sighed. I wanted to tell him to get lost, but I couldn't. Damien was the love of my life. He was my everything. I couldn't turn my back on him no matter how badly I wanted to.

"I have this new script, Lyric. We're going to get back on top." Damien's voice seeped through the space at the bottom of the bathroom door.

"I hope so, Damien." Tissue in hand, I emerged from my sanctuary. "I really hope so."

Stepping into the hall, I took a quick look around the urban contemporary mansion with gold posts and marble floors. In a matter of sixty days, my beautiful home was going to become property of the bank. I hadn't paid the mortgage in almost a year. It wasn't due to neglect. I simply couldn't afford it. Our house payment was a whopping thirty grand a month. Add that to the children's private school tuition, car notes, other bills,

groceries, as well as my and Damien's parents' mort-
gages, I was almost $6 million in debt. The sum once
sounded like pennies to us young millionaires. Now a
bitch was practically counting pennies to keep the lights
on and food in the fridge.

"Just have faith in me," Damien pleaded. "I know I'll
land this one."

"I have faith, Damien," I lied with a straight face, only
saying what he wanted to hear because that was who I
was. What I wanted to tell him was that my faith in him
died the last time he snorted a line of cocaine.

On the other hand, I did have faith in myself. The last
few years had been rough, but I had a few tricks up my
sleeve. This hood chick from Boston still knew how to
make a dollar out of fifteen cents. Where I came from,
only the fittest survived. Dammit, I was a survivor—always had been, always would be.

# Chapter Six

## *Jasmine*

I grabbed the prenatal vitamins that Dr. Shiloh had left atop the counter, looked at them, then tossed them into my purse. Next, I slid on my black spandex pants and pulled up my tan and brown Coach rain boots. I gave myself the once-over in the large mirror that was hanging on the wall. Staring at my reflection, I wondered why I felt so ugly and empty inside. According to most people, I was a pretty girl. My skin tone was that of creamy caramel. My eyes were almond shaped, and my lips were full. I was five feet four inches and weighed a sexy 140 pounds. Had I been a little taller, I probably could've been a model. But right now, I felt like a rag doll.

Blinking rapidly, I shook the somber mood off. I had to pull myself together. Therefore, I said a quick prayer, grabbed my gold LV bag, and was out the door in seconds. I blew through the pastel pink lobby that was full of women with my head buried down in my purse. My long Malaysian hair extensions covered the sides of my face as I pretended to be searching for something. I was not trying to be noticed by a KJ fan who recognized me from a television special or magazine spread. I was also ducking the paparazzi who made it their business to be all up in my shit every day, all day. Now that KJ was famous, my life had become an open book, and I didn't need any attention today, especially not up in the fucking gynecologist's office.

"Hey, girl, where did you park?" I called my best friend, Stacey, as I scanned the parking lot for her cranberry-colored Chrysler 300. She was acting as my assistant and chauffeur for the day.

"Damn, bitch, put your glasses on. I'm right here in front of the door." She laughed. I laughed too because she was indeed parked less than ten steps away from me. I hustled over to the car and gave her the middle finger. Her dumb ass was leaning on the car horn, and people were starting to stare at us.

"Stace, cut that shit out." I laughed.

"They say if you can't see, then you must definitely be able to hear. I blew the horn so that your blind ass could find your way to the car." Stacey started up the car, then pulled out of the parking lot. We rode in silence for about eight minutes until Stacey spoke again. "Damn, what's wrong with you?" she asked as we merged onto the 696 freeway.

"You already know." I rolled my eyes because I knew she was about to go ham on my ass. Stacey wasn't your average friend. This bitch kept it one hundred even when you didn't want her to. We'd been friends ever since middle school, and I loved her like a sister. She was my main bitch for real.

"Jasmine, don't tell me you're pregnant again." She shook her head with a disappointed expression plastered on her face.

"All right, then, I won't." I shifted in my seat. She looked over at me in disbelief. Out of shame and embarrassment, I looked away.

"Fuck that, Jas. You are definitely having this motherfucking baby. Your ass can't keep getting abortions, girl. King is just going to have to understand." Her mind was made up for me. I wished it were that simple, but it wasn't.

"You know how King feels about more babies," I said, getting choked up because I really did want another child.

"Fuck King!" she shouted, causing me to jump slightly. "It ain't like that nigga is even home anyway, and when his ass is home, he doesn't ever kick it with Jordan. You could be out here getting loose with his money like some of the other hip-hop wives we know. They're out asking for liposuction, tummy tucks, cars, and houses. Shit, all you want is a damn baby! It seems to me that he shouldn't mind having another child if it's something you want to do. I mean, it's not like y'all broke and can't afford it. Hell, even broke niggas in the hood be having 'bout six, seven kids, trying to dodge child support like the police." She laughed.

Just then my iPhone vibrated. "Hello," I answered without peeping the caller ID.

"What up, Jazzy? Where you at?" King spoke loudly into the phone. There was a bunch of noise in his background. I could tell he was at the airport. They were calling gate numbers and announcing delays over the loudspeaker.

"I'm in the car with Stacey. What's up?" I put my index finger inside my free ear so that I could hear him better.

"I told you about hanging with that bitch. You will listen one day." He smacked his lips.

I glanced over at Stace to see if she had heard him. Her expression didn't change, so I kept on talking. "Where are you, baby?"

"I'm at the airport in Dallas. Something happened with the jet. They're working on it, but it won't be fixed until tomorrow. I told the label that I was ready to get the fuck home, so me and D-Bo about to hop on the next thing smoking back to the D."

"Yay," I squealed. My man had been on location at a movie set for the past five months. I had only seen him approximately six times during that entire stretch, so I was anxious. "Baby, what time does your flight land? I want to be at the airport with Jordan to pick you up."

"Damn, baby, I'm on standby. I don't know what time I'll be home because I don't know what flight I'm leaving on." He paused. "I'll just see you when I get there, and you better have that pretty pussy trimmed up and waiting for me."

"You know I keep my shit tight all the time." I giggled, and Stacey rolled her eyes.

"I know you do, Jazzy. Yo' shit is on point! That's why you're my wife. Now go buy yourself something sexy, and I'll see your fine ass sometime tonight."

"Love you." I blew a kiss through the phone, then ended the call.

"Ugh." Stacey gagged.

"What?" I asked my girl, who was giving me the screw face.

"Nothing, girl. Don't mind me and my disdain for your nigga." She waved a dismissive hand and shook her head. I hunched my shoulders, reclined in the seat, and closed my eyes before I said something I would later regret.

Although I knew Stacey had my best interests at heart, sometimes I wished she would stay out of my business. A lot of outsiders viewed Stacey as a hater, but I knew otherwise. She had no reason to hate because she was a beautiful girl who resembled the model Tyra Banks— smile, skin tone, height, and all. The men in the music industry flocked to her whenever she attended an event with me. I knew for a fact that she had gotten down with a few of them and even still remained fuck buddies with at least one on the YMCMB label. Hate wasn't the reason she disliked KJ, and I knew it. Stacey had been my girl since way back and had played witness to the good, bad, and ugly shit happening in my life. She was always my shoulder to cry on after fights with King. She also lent me her ears when I needed a sounding board. All in all, she was my dog. I just wished she would lighten up on King.

"So I guess you aren't hanging with me and Tracey tonight like you promised," Stacey reminded me, causing my eyes to pop open. I had completely forgotten that tonight was part one of a birthday celebration for Stacey and her twin sister, Tracey. Today was actually her sister's birthday, being that she was born at 11:59 p.m. Stacey was born the next day at 12:01 a.m. For that reason, they always had a two-day celebration.

"Damn, Stace, I totally forgot just that quick." I felt awful. I knew she thought I was putting her off for my man once again.

"It's cool. Don't even worry about it." She brushed me off.

"Stace, don't play me like that. You know I haven't seen King in a while. Truth be told, you would do the same in a heartbeat if one of those thugs you were fucking with went to jail for a stretch and was finally coming home." I smiled and Stace did too. She knew I was right.

"Whatever, bitch." She flipped me the finger, and I blew her a kiss.

"You know what, Stace? I might just have a plan."

"I'm listening." She cut on her blinker to signal her left turn.

"King doesn't know what time he'll get home. It will probably be late. I'm going to come to the party, then leave a little early and be home before he gets back." When I said that, she smiled. "Now before you go getting all happy and shit, remember I probably won't be at your party tomorrow night. It all depends on how King is feeling," I warned so she wouldn't act brand new if I didn't show up.

"Okay, that's cool. As long as you can party with me tonight, it's all good," she said, then turned up her sound system. We bumped the new August Alsina album all the way to Tracey's house.

Stacey blew the horn, and out popped Tracey on the phone looking ghetto fabulous. Tracey's ass was a bona fide hood rat. Yet she somehow managed to acquire and maintain some really nice things. For instance, this girl hadn't had a job in a month of Sundays, but she was driving a 2014 Jaguar. She lived in a plush townhome in a newly developed subdivision, and her gear was always fresh to death.

"Trick, stop blowing. I hear you. I got neighbors," she called to her sister, then turned around to lock her front door.

"Hey, Jasmine, can I hold a dollar?" Tracey's 8-year-old son, Prince, approached the car with his hand out. I smiled at the little handsome boy, who was the spitting image of his mom.

"Oooh, me too! Can I get a dollar?" Princess, Tracey's 3-year-old daughter, asked. Reaching inside my purse, I was about to hand both of them $5 bills. However, Tracey pulled them away from the car with an attitude.

"What I tell y'all about asking people for their money? Get in the car with Grandma," she scolded them as she ushered them toward a gray Ford Focus that was parked in her driveway.

"I didn't know your mom was over here. Let's get out and speak to her," I suggested to Stacey.

"You go ahead. I'm good. That old bitch ain't trying to talk to me." She smacked her lips.

"Damn, why you say that?" I asked with my hand on the door handle.

"She always has her damn hand out, that's why. I work too hard for mine, so I don't put nothing in her greasy palms. Somehow Tracey gets her money easy, and she keeps my mom happy. Needless to say, my mama is team Tracey all the way." Stace rolled her eyes.

I nodded my understanding and stepped from the car. I walked up to the door of the Focus and tapped lightly. "Hey, Mama," I said as she opened her door and stepped out for a hug.

"Hey, Jasmine, look at you." Her voice was raspy like Frankie's, Keyshia Cole's mother. "You still look good, girl. That man of yours still rapping?"

"Yes, ma'am." I smiled proudly.

"Is the money still right?" She winked.

"Uh, yes, ma'am," I replied.

"That's good." She nodded and cut to the chase. "Can I hold something then?"

"How much you need?" I asked cautiously.

"How much you got?" She posed in a B-boy stance, arms crossed and feet spread apart.

"I only have about forty dollars in cash. The rest is all on my credit cards," I said honestly.

"Okay, Jasmine, it was nice talking to ya." She dismissed me and got back into her car, letting the door slam and rolling her window up.

*Well, damn.*

# Chapter Seven

## *Tionne*

Standing out in the pouring rain, I hit the lock on the black Mercedes G-Wagen parked near the fountain in my driveway and hopped in. For a second, I just stared at my reflection in the rearview mirror. I looked like shit, but I felt liberated. For the first time in a long time, I was free, no longer giving a fuck about image or what people thought about me. My mother used to tell me that if a nigga wasn't paying my bills, then fuck 'im. I used to laugh then, but now I was taking heed.

With no destination in mind, I hit the gate control in my whip and watched as the ten-foot wrought iron gates opened. Instantly, a mob of photographers began snapping pictures.

"Where are you going, Tionne?"

"Why don't you have on any clothing?"

"Where is Dallas?"

I didn't respond to a single question while revving the engine. Just as I prepared to pull off, my front door opened. I half expected Dallas to come chasing me down. However, I wasn't prepared for what I saw. This nigga was hurling my belongings out the front door piece by piece. At first, I tried to pay it no mind, but the more my shit came flying out of the house, the more pissed off I got.

"What are you doing?" I yelled.

"I'm sick of your games, Tionne. If you want to leave, then leave," Dallas said before tossing a box of Louboutins at me.

"So you're in the wrong, but you mad because I'm leaving?" I jumped from the car, completely oblivious to the paparazzi having a field day.

"Tionne, I give you everything and you still ain't happy. So fuck it. I'm done," he barked.

"You're done? No, nigga, I'm done." Barging past him, I entered through the front door and opened the coat closet.

"What are you doing?" Now Dallas was behind me.

"I can show you better than I can tell you." *Bingo*. I spotted a set of golf clubs he used at a charity event, and I pulled out the 9 iron. "You want to damage my shit?" I laughed. "Okay, I got you."

"Girl, you better not do what I think you're about to do." Dallas's eyes were as big as saucers.

"You better get out of my way." I swung the club in his direction, intentionally avoiding his head.

With Dallas on my heels, I entered the kitchen and started busting out the glass windows on each cabinet. Next, I swung the golf club down and took to severely damaging the granite countertops.

"What the fuck, Tionne?"

I took my tirade into the family room, which was attached to the kitchen. Lining the walls were several Grammys and VMAs.

"Don't do it," Dallas yelled just before I resumed my crusade. Things went flying in every direction. After I cleared the wall, Dallas once again tried to stop me, but he was no match for my speed. I ducked under his arm and headed into his office.

"Tionne, you better cut this shit out right now!" Dallas ran up behind me.

With the laugh of a crazy woman, I raised the club above my head, then swung it with all my might. It was with immense gratification that I watched Dallas's first framed platinum album shatter into pieces.

"Are you fucking crazy?" Struggling to salvage his most prized possession, Dallas pushed past me.

I didn't know why, but out of nowhere I started crying. "Dallas, why can't you just be right? Don't you know how much I love you? Don't you know how much I've given to this relationship?" I whimpered. "I love you more than I love myself sometimes. Why can't you just do right by me?"

"Tionne, I do love you, and I want to be right, baby, I do, but . . ." Dallas took a seat in his desk chair, then lowered his head in shame.

"Am I not good enough?" I continued to tear up. For years, the question stayed etched in my mind, but I dared not ask it for fear of the answer.

"Tionne, you are good enough. I'm just too stupid to realize it at times." Dallas stood and came over to embrace me. "I'm a flawed man who has made my fair share of mistakes, but if you can give me one more chance, I swear on my father's grave, I'll try to do better."

"Dallas, do you know how many chances you've been given?" I pushed away from him. "I love you but I'm leaving."

"Please don't leave me." Dallas recognized that this time I was serious. I could tell he was scared to death.

"You and I both know this ain't working, so let's stop pretending." I'd come to this conclusion a long time ago but finally found the strength to act.

"Baby, I'll get my shit together. I don't want to lose you." Dallas was practically begging.

Normally, I would find this amusing, but today I was over it. "I'm tired of being lied to and cheated on. I know you're tired of cheating and getting caught, so let's make it easy on both of us," I sighed before turning toward the door.

"Tionne, I can't live without you, ma."

"At one time, I thought that was true, Dallas, but you'll survive. Trust me." Smiling, I exited the room, then made my way to the front door, which was still wide open.

"Are you leaving for a few days or filing for a divorce?" Dallas sounded like a saddened child.

"I'm gone for good, baby." For the second time that night, I raised my right hand and chucked him the deuces. "It's time to do me."

"Baby, please, think about giving us another try."

"The straw that broke the camel's back was the call I received the other day from the gynecologist." I turned to face him. "You gave me chlamydia."

"What?" Dallas looked dumbfounded.

"That's right, nigga. You don't even love me enough to use a rubber." Without another word, I kept on walking.

On the way out, I spotted a red Cavalli one-piece lying on the floor and slipped it on. Dallas was still behind me. However, he remained quiet. Until now, I had never made good on my threats to leave. He was shocked but I wasn't. I had reached my breaking point. Therefore, I was done with a capital D. A bitch felt like Angela Bassett in the movie *Waiting to Exhale* when she lit the car on fire.

As I walked away, my adrenaline level was rising. Yet I was as cool as a cucumber when I stepped outside my house. The paparazzi were still there snapping pictures, fetching for a story, but I didn't care. After hopping behind the wheel of the waiting G-Wagen, I put the pedal to the metal, then sped off into my new life. "Fuck *Love & Hip Hop.*"

# Chapter Eight

## *Jasmine*

"I mean, why we have to go all the way out to Somerset Mall?" Tracey whined from the back seat.

"Because Jasmine is the one paying for my shit, and that's where she wants to go." Stacey tried to shut her sister down, but Tracey wasn't having it.

"Fuck that! It's my birthday. The bitch ain't buying my shit, and I want to go somewhere else." She pouted like a child.

"Take me home before I have to fuck your sister up," I demanded. I didn't know what her deal was. Ever since King got signed and we moved out of the hood, Tracey and I had had beef. It was like she was mad that we made it.

"I ain't taking nobody home," Stacey said to me. "T, you're right. It's your birthday. Where do you want to go?" she said, siding with her sister.

I looked at her and rolled my eyes. Wherever it was, I just hoped this hood bitch picked a decent spot. I wanted to do my friend proper for her birthday, and I couldn't do that at some flea market–type shit.

"Let's roll over to Uniquely Different. It's a new spot in Oak Park, and it's all that," Tracey gushed.

I'd been there before. She was right, the place was popping, but I had to wonder how she could even afford to shop there. I was aware that she dated a few dope boys from time to time, but no one consistent, and I seriously doubted some nigga just looking for a booty call was footing the bill. Hopefully, she wouldn't try to steal anything, because I was not going to bail her ass out.

We walked into the establishment like three women on a mission. "Hello. Welcome to Uniquely Different. I'm Diane. What can I help you with today?" asked a tall, redheaded, middle-aged white woman with a short, razor-cut bob.

"It's my best friend's birthday. I want her to look fabulous at her party tonight, and price is no object. What's new in your collection?" I asked while Tracey walked off to do her own thing.

"I have a custom Gianni Santana piece that was just flown in yesterday," Diane said with a huge grin on her face. Pulling us toward the back showroom, she grabbed a few catalogs, showed us a few pieces, then left us alone to try some things on.

"Do you see this place?" Stacey asked from her dressing room.

"Yes. This is top of the line," I added. The boutique was to die for, starting with the crystal chandeliers and chic hot pink and silver wallpaper and ending with the black lacquer fixtures and gray plush carpet.

"Let me see you," I called out to my girl.

"I'm about to kill them softly with this one." Stace emerged from the dressing room wearing a royal blue skintight minidress. The neckline plunged, and the back was barely there. It was that dress, and in it, she was that bitch.

"Oh, Stace, I'm loving it, boo. I have some blue suede Christian Louboutins that would go perfect with that dress."

"This dress is fifteen hundred dollars." Stace peeked a look at the price tag.

"It's all good. You know you're worth every dollar." I smiled. "I'm going to find something for you to wear tomorrow at your party. It's going to be a surprise, and you can't open it until then, okay?" She nodded, and then I walked away to find my gift.

As I looked around the store, I noticed Tracey carrying three dresses and a box of shoes to the register. I tried not to be too nosy, but it was what it was, so fuck it.

"Your total today comes to $6,280.17. Will you be paying with cash or credit?" the cashier asked. I was outdone and about to pass the hell out. How in the hell was this girl getting her money?

"Credit," she said, blowing me away. Cash was one thing, but to have a credit card with that much on it was shocking for her. Somebody was keeping this bitch. I wondered who it was.

I went on about my business of browsing and finally stumbled across a red satin dress with one strap and a pleated bottom. This was the one, so I went to the register to pay for it. My total for the two dresses and accessories that Stacey had picked out was only $4,090.52. I handed the woman my card and waited for my receipt.

"You didn't get nothing for yourself, Miss High and Mighty?" Tracey asked from behind me.

"Nope. Today is all about my girl." I brushed her off. This chick was not about to take me out of character in this fine establishment.

"Is that so?" She raised an arched eyebrow. "Or you just can't afford to?" Tracey added on the sly.

"First of all, hood rat, I don't need nothing right now because my man just sent me on a shopping spree in Italy last month. Second of all, don't act like you be balling on the regular because you just spent six Gs. Lastly, don't fuck around and get your ass beat on your birthday," I said, squaring up to her. The bitch had me by several inches, but I wasn't about to back down. She wanted to go there, so I served it up proper. With everything on my mind, I would've whooped her ass in an instant before God could even get the news.

"You think you the only one who can have a baby and get a payday?" she said.

"I never looked at it like that, but yeah, I guess I do." I smiled. "Your dusty ass has two babies and still no payday! Is that why you're salty? As a matter of fact, where in the hell are your baby daddies anyway?" I got her with that one.

"My kids' daddy"—she put emphasis on the fact that both her kids shared the same father—"is minding his fucking paper."

"Is that so?"

"You think you're all that and something special, don't you?" Looking me over from top to bottom, Tracey paid close attention to the $3,000 hair on my head and my frosted ears, neck, and wrist. The bitch almost gagged when her eyes landed on my ten-carat princess-cut chocolate stone. "I want you to know that I could've had KJ if I wanted him, but I didn't," was her comeback.

"Then explain why I'm the one with the ring." I extended my hand for good measure. She rolled her eyes and walked out of the store.

The rest of the evening went smoothly. Tracey stayed in her lane, and I stayed in mine. Besides, I was only there to ensure my bestie was having a ball. By the looks of it, she was partying like a rock star. I had bottle after bottle of Moët Rosé sent over to the table. I wasn't drinking, but it was my girl's favorite drink, and I didn't want her to go empty. I danced on a few songs, wished my girl a happy birthday, and was out before they rolled in the cake. I needed to beat King home. By the time on my watch, I was pushing it. I had a little over an hour to get from downtown to the suburbs, shower, and get changed.

With no time to waste, my ass was whipping my black Lincoln Navigator onto I-75. Dodging in and out of traffic, I finally pulled up to my gate. "Shit," I said aloud when I noticed King waiting for me on the walkway. I glanced down at the time. It read 11:15 p.m., which was thirty minutes away from the time King was due to arrive home. I had gotten a text from him hours ago confirming his expected arrival. I guessed either the plane had landed early or he was lying about the time to catch me slipping.

"Hey, baby." I stepped from the SUV cautiously.

"Where you been?" He mugged me.

"Oh, I forgot it was Stacey and Tracey's birthday party tonight. You know that's my best friend, so I couldn't miss it." I leaned in for a kiss, but he turned away.

"Where did I ask you to be?" His jaw muscles tightened.

"Baby, you said you'd be back here just before midnight. I figured I could go to the party, stay for an hour or two, leave, and be home when you got here." I shrugged my shoulders. "I just wanted to make everybody happy."

"Fuck making everybody happy. I'm your man, your number one priority." He pointed at himself.

"King, I'm sorry," I tried to apologize.

"Yes, you are, Jasmine. You are one sorry mother-fucker." He turned, then walked toward the house.

Watching him walk away, I stood there in shock. On one hand, I couldn't believe King was acting like this. Then again, I could. This wasn't my first time being dis-respected by him. As a matter of fact, it'd been happening so frequently that I was rarely surprised anymore when-ever it happened. I didn't feel like chasing after him, so I sat on the stone staircase, removed my heels, set them to the side, and put my head down in my lap. My life was going nowhere fast, and I needed to do something quick.

"Hey there, baby girl," I heard my mother say from behind me.

"Hey, Mama. Thanks for watching Jordan for me." I slid over as she sat beside me.

"That's my grandbaby. Thank you isn't needed." She put her arms around me. "Are you okay?"

"I'm good. I just hate the way he treats me sometimes. It's like I can't do anything right. He makes me feel so worthless at times." I exhaled as she rubbed my back.

"Baby, a man will only treat you the way you allow him to. I see a lot of things around here I don't like, but it's not my place to say anything. You're his wife, and you signed up for this. Nobody can tell you what to do in your marriage. It's up to you. You have to decide when you've had enough, baby girl. Mama can't hold your hand through everything."

She kissed my forehead. I loved my mother to death and was her spitting image. To this day, we were mistaken for sisters. Minus a few wrinkles, give or take a few pounds, my mama could still hang with the best of them. She put her life on hold to help me care for Jordan. I appreciated her so much. Without her support, I didn't know what I would have done during the rough nights when my son cried for hours. She was there during his many doctor appointments and hospital stays, always reassuring me that everything would be okay.

"So are you going to stay out there all night?" King's voice boomed from the patio of our second-floor master suite.

I looked at my mama, and then she squeezed me tightly before standing to leave.

"Thanks, Mama. I love you," I said and watched her until she was safely inside her 2014 Chevy Camaro.

After checking in on Jordan and finding him asleep in his hospital bed, I walked next door into our bedroom. "Damn, 'bout time you came in the house." King was lying across the triple king-sized bed in nothing but Polo boxers.

"What's up, baby?" I crawled across the bed and snuggled up next to him. "How was your flight?"

"It was cool. I'm just glad to be home lying in this bed next to you." He nibbled on my neck.

"I'm glad you're home too, baby. We missed you," I said seductively.

"What did you miss most about me?" His erect eight inches of man candy popped up suddenly. King's soldier wanted some attention, and I knew exactly what to do. Without saying a word, I slid down to the bottom of the bed and went to work.

"Damn, baby," my man moaned, which turned me on. "Suck that shit, Jazzy, just like that, baby."

"You like this, baby?" I licked around the head of his penis.

"You know I do. Stop talking and keep sucking." He pushed my head down farther until I began to gag.

"King, baby, I can't go that deep." My eyes watered up, and I began to cough.

"Baby, you better get your skull game up before I find a replacement," he joked.

"Whatever. I'm not going anywhere. Me and you will be together forever." I got up from the bed and walked toward the spa-like bathroom.

"With head like that, you'll be lucky if I'm here when you come back from the bathroom." He grabbed the remote and turned on the television. Removing my dress, I tossed it at him playfully.

# Chapter Nine

## *Zuri*

The next morning, I was greeted by the smell of breakfast as well as the sound of running bathwater. Part of Jason's ritual was to provide me with ladies-in-waiting, gifts, and a personal masseuse the day after he roughed me up. There was a total of three women contracted to run my bath, cook, and pamper me. I didn't have to lift a finger if I didn't want to.

"Mrs. Armstrong, your bath awaits you," Karen, one of the ladies-in-waiting, spoke from the doorway.

"I'll be there in a second," I replied with a groan. My body felt like shit, and I was certain it looked the same. I didn't have to see the bruises near my stomach to know they were there.

"I took the liberty of adding in your favorite lavender scent," Karen declared with a smile.

"Thank you," I stated before standing my nude self from the bed and heading toward the 400-square-foot master en suite equipped with a vanity area, four-head shower, and two-person steam room.

"Hopefully, the water is to your liking."

"It's perfect," I replied after dipping my finger into the oversized oval tub sitting in the center of the floor.

With Karen's assistance, I stepped into the tub and practically melted into the warm water. Bubbles were filled to the brim just the way I liked it. "I'll leave you to rest, Mrs. Armstrong, but I'm just outside the door if you need me." With a bow, Karen backed out of the bathroom and left me to my thoughts.

Slowly, I lifted my head toward the mirror on the ceiling to assess the damage done to my body. As I suspected, Jason's handprint was still slightly visible around my neck, and my face was swollen. However, it wasn't too bad, nothing a little makeup wouldn't conceal.

"Thank God," I mumbled to myself before leaning back into the bathtub. Things could've been much worse. I was thankful they weren't. I remembered one time Jason had broken my nose and dislocated my shoulder. That was, by far, the worse beatdown I had received at the hands of my husband.

"Zuri." I heard Syl before she entered the bathroom. "What the hell is going on around here? Who are all of these people?" The look on her face was pure confusion.

"It's your son's way of apologizing," I replied before closing my eyes, laying my head back, then slipping down farther into the tub. The water practically covered my ears.

"Fuck that. He needs to be taking his sorry ass to anger management," she yelled.

"It doesn't happen that often," I conveyed with my eyes still closed. However, I could imagine Syl pacing back and forth in need of a cigarette although she had quit almost two years ago.

"One time is too many, Zuri. What in the fuck is wrong with you?"

"Let it go." I was trying my best to remain polite. I knew she was only trying to help me, but it was what it was. If I had learned to accept it, she should too.

"What about Jelly?" Syl asked.

My eyes popped open with the quickness. Her question caught me off guard. "What about her?"

"Is this the kind of example you want to set for your daughter? Believe it or not, you're telling her it's okay to let a man put his hands on you as long as his pockets are deep."

"Sylvia, Jelly has nothing to do with my choices. As long as she is well-fed and taken care of, it shouldn't matter what's going on in my personal life." Unintentionally, my voice had risen an octave, but I was furious with my mother-in-law for mentioning my daughter.

"Right now, Jelly is a baby, totally oblivious to the go-ings-on around here. Eventually, she'll grow up. What do you think will happen when she begins to see the violence for herself? What do you think will happen when she's the one picking you up off the floor time and time again?"

I didn't respond, so Syl continued. "Jelly is going to go right out and find a man just like her father! Oh, just forget it." Visibly upset, Syl smacked her lips and left the room. I was glad, too, because I was tired of talking. Deep down inside, I knew Syl was right, but what could I do? My hands were tied.

"Are you ready for me to wash your back?"

I nodded. Smiling, Karen reentered the bathroom, holding all the things needed for my bath.

Twenty minutes later, I was in my bedroom standing before the massive walk-in closet with eight-foot doors and its own security camera. Everything inside was a name brand and considerably expensive. Some of the pieces were custom made, one of a kind. Some items I had only worn once or never worn at all. As my eyes scanned the room, I was immediately drawn in by a yel-low ensemble with a feathery train. I was wearing it the night I walked in Roberto Cavalli's fashion show in Paris.

It was a big night for both me and Jason. His sports representation agency had just secured the next king of the NBA. We were on cloud nine until Jason's former best friend, Forty Shades, went on a rampage calling him out about not being smart enough to graduate from high school. It was a secret that Jason never wanted to get out. He was mortified by the betrayal of his boy, but he took it out on me.

After the show, we went back to the hotel to change for the after-party. One thing led to another, and Jason began beating me like I had stolen something. As usual, I said nothing. Not because I didn't want to, but because his massive hand covered my mouth. When the brutality was over, he grabbed my shoes and purse, then tossed them at me. When my purse hit the floor, a pregnancy stick spilled out. Silently, Jason grabbed it and read the positive results. Immediately, he tried to apologize, but it was too late. We both knew the damage had been done as we watched the blood flow from between my legs.

Lulu, my second lady-in-waiting, called from the door, "Mrs. Armstrong, your food is waiting."

"Give me a second." I sniffled before grabbing a YSL sweat suit off the shelf and slamming the closet door.

On the way downstairs, I checked in on my daughter, who was still asleep in her pink princess toddler bed. Looking down at her precious face caused tears to pour down my face for two reasons. The first was that I was so grateful I hadn't endured any violence while I carried her, because I would've lost her too. The second reason was due to what Syl expressed. The thought of someone putting their hands on my baby girl nearly drove me crazy. They say history repeats itself. I would never want Jelly to be a man's punching bag.

"Mrs. Armstrong, your breakfast is getting cold." Lulu popped her head in the door.

"I'm coming." I dabbed the corner of my eyes, then headed for the kitchen.

As soon as I descended the spiral staircase, I noticed several boxes lining the edge of each stair, twenty in total. They were arranged from smallest to largest and were all wrapped in Tiffany blue wrapping paper.

"Someone must love you very much!" Lulu commented while stopping to hand me the first box.

"I guess," I replied while tearing into the gift. It was a pair of sapphire earrings trimmed with diamonds. The second box was the matching necklace, the third a matching ring, and the fourth was, of course, the matching bracelet. The next set of boxes contained clothing, shoes, and purses. Toward the end of the staircase, I unwrapped two boxes with mink coats. The very last gift was the largest. It really had my attention. The boy had practically given me everything except another car.

"I wonder what it is." Lulu was more excited than I was.

"I don't have a clue." With a jolt of excitement, I bent down and shook the box. A few weeks ago, I mentioned getting a puppy. Maybe this was it. However, nothing moved in the box, and I didn't hear any noise coming from it. Quickly, I pulled the ribbon, then tore into the paper with the nail of my index finger. Curiosity was killing both me and Lulu. Her eyes were as big as saucers.

"Oh, my God," I screamed. Resting inside the box were several neat stacks of cash. Atop the large pile of money was an envelope. "This has to be at least sixty thousand dollars," I said to no one in particular.

"Open the letter," Lulu urged. Inside was a note, which I read aloud.

*Zuri,*
*Grab a few friends and take them on a trip on me,*
*all expenses paid.*
*Jay*

It was just like my husband not to even apologize. Sure, the gesture was nice, and the gifts were excellent, but not once had he said he was sorry for hurting me.

"You're so lucky, Mrs. Armstrong." Lulu shook her head in admiration.

I wanted to remind Lulu about all the bruises she'd help me nurse over the years and tell her that luck had nothing to do with this. I had earned every fucking thing he gave me plus more. Nevertheless, I smiled as I always did and remained silent.

# Chapter Ten

## *Lyric*

"Good luck today, baby," I yelled out of the window at Damien before I pulled out of the driveway. Today was his big audition. I was praying like hell things went well. We needed it.

"Mom, can we order a pizza tonight?" Jonah asked from the back seat.

"We ain't got no money for a pizza," Leslie replied before I could say anything.

"Are we poor, Mommy? Leslie said we're poor."

Jonah's words almost made me choke. "Leslie, why would you say that?" I looked at my daughter with a puckered brow.

"That's what I saw online," Leslie replied with a whisper.

"Didn't I tell you about not reading and believing everything on the internet?"

"Yeah, but my friends are always showing me stuff. They said we're poor and Daddy is a drug addict."

"Fuck your friends!" I spat before I knew it. Immediately, the car was silent. "Look, I'm sorry. I didn't mean to say that." Sighing, I decided that it was time to have a heart-to-heart with my children. As much as I wanted to shelter them from our situation, I couldn't. "Listen, guys, things have been tight for us, I'm not going to lie, but we are not poor."

"So why do the internet blogs say it?" Leslie looked at me.

"Sometimes, the media has a way of bending the truth for public enjoyment. They put out lies and gossip about celebrity personas because it makes their company more popular."

"So why can't we just get online and tell them it's not true?" This time it was Jonah asking the questions.

"Baby, we can't fight them all, so it's better to just leave it alone. Eventually, they will find someone else to pick on, and our story will be old news." Although I was smiling, I wanted to cry so badly. It was one thing to talk about me and Damien. I could handle that. But when it started affecting my children, my feelings were on a whole other level. "Listen, guys, I promise things will get better and this too shall pass, okay? The money and the fame may come and go, but as long as our family stays together, that's all that matters, right?"

"Yes, ma'am," they replied in unison just as we pulled up to their school. This had been the longest ten-minute ride to school ever.

"You guys have a good day, and I'll pick up two pizzas tonight, okay, Jonah?"

"Cool. Thanks, Mom." Jonah gave me a kiss on the cheek.

"Bye, Mom." Leslie smiled before jumping out of the car.

I watched until my kids were in the building before releasing the brake. Just as I did, Mrs. Clementine, the head of the school, flagged me down.

"Fuck," I snarled under my breath.

"Mrs. Robertson, did Leslie tell you that without her tuition she won't be able to partake in today's field trip?"

"Her tuition is in her book bag. Sorry I forgot." I tried to pull off again.

"Did you send Jonah's as well?" Mrs. Clementine continued.

"No, actually I didn't. I'll send his next week."

"Mrs. Robertson, let me remind you that our waiting list is very long. When you enrolled your children, you were made aware that their tuition was due no later than the end of first semester. We're nearing the end of third semester. If you don't have it, please don't hold up spaces for children with funds."

I couldn't believe this bitch had the audacity to come at me the way she did. The newly refined Lyric would've nodded her understanding, then pulled off. However, the old B-More Lyric was the one behind the wheel today. If this lady wanted to start shit, I was about to serve it proper. Putting the car in park, I opened the door and stepped out.

"Look, Valerie," I said, addressing her by her first name, "I don't know who the fuck you think you are to be coming at me sideways, but let me inform you that I'm not the one to be talked to like a child," I snapped. "So what I missed the due date on the fucking tuition? My children have been coming here for years, and this is the first time it has happened. Second of all, you're failing to remember all of the money my husband and I have donated to this goddamn school. Third of all, if you ever—and I do mean ever—talk slick and address me in that manner again, I will not hesitate to whoop your ass." I was on ten, totally oblivious to the crowd of parents and paparazzi watching and recording the scene word for word.

"Well, I see you can take the girl out of the ghetto, but you can't take the ghetto out of the girl," Valerie replied.

"Oh, I'm going to show you ghetto," I warned.

"You lay one hand on me, and I won't hesitate to expel your children and sue you for whatever you have left." She readjusted the jacket on her too-tight gray suit, then turned on the balls of her kitten heels and retreated toward the safety of the school.

"Care to comment on what just happened, Lyric?" One of the reporters stuck his camera in my face. In a fit of rage, I didn't hesitate to swing at him. He dodged me. I was glad he did. Had I hit him or damaged his camera, I would've paid dearly. It was time to get the fuck out of here.

"Move," I screamed while pushing past the nosy bystanders. Hopping back inside of my car, I put the pedal to the metal, then sped off.

After I rode twenty minutes in silence to my appointment, the Bluetooth in my car rang. The caller ID read my mother's name. At first, I started not to pick up but decided against it. "Hello, Mother."

"Hey, pooh." She sounded as if life were perfect. I guessed it was for her when she didn't have a care in the world. Everything she owned I was footing the bill for.

"What's up?"

"I was calling because your father and I are celebrating fifty years in two months, and I thought it would be great to have a little party to celebrate."

"Mom, I really—"

"I was thinking maybe you could rent out the ballroom at the country club, and we could invite at least fifty of our closest friends and church members." She rambled on as if this had been planned for months.

"Mom, I just—"

"That number doesn't include family, so it'll be approximately two hundred. My favorite color is cream, and your father's is brown. Maybe that could be the theme," she continued without pause. "I took the liberty of calling Changa, and we set up a meeting for this Friday."

Changa was an event specialist I used from time to time, and he was quite pricey. "How are you paying for this?" I asked, realizing that would quiet her down.

"Huh?" she asked, obviously dumbfounded.

"I'm on a budget, and I can't afford to throw you and Daddy a lavish party right now." Even though this was the first time I was telling my mother no, I knew she wouldn't like it.

"I never ask you for anything, and the one time I do, you turn me down?" She sounded outdone. I wanted to remind her that while she hadn't asked me for anything, it didn't stop me from paying her mortgage, buying her and my father's car, and sending them a monthly allowance as well as sending them on lavish vacations twice a year.

"Mom, we're going through some financial issues right now. If something changes, I will cover the party. If not, I just can't."

"Mm-hmm," my mother said before smacking her lips. Her reaction was a little hurtful. A mother should've been more caring and understanding. She should've asked me if there was anything she could do instead of being self-ish. Sadly, I learned a long time ago that money changed people for the worse. The minute Damien hit it big, I began to hear from people I hadn't spoken to in years. Family members began to call with all kinds of sob stories, and friends started changing.

"Look, Mom, I have to go. I'll call you later." I ended the call and pulled over to the side of the road. The tears in my eyes had taken over, and I could no longer see. Silently, I sobbed until I had nothing left. I was tired of everything and everybody. I just needed some me time before I went crazy, but that wasn't going to happen anytime soon.

Seconds after getting myself together, I pulled up and pressed the call button on my client's gate opener.

"Come on in, Lyric," Ken replied and buzzed me in. He had been my client ever since he joined the NBA. I normally supplied him with suits for press conferences or streetwear, but today he had put in a request for women's clothing.

After grabbing my garment bags from the rear of my whip, I headed up to Ken's condominium. He was standing in the doorway wearing a small white tee, brown man capri pants, and a pair of canvas gym shoes. "There's my girl with the goods." He stepped aside and permitted me to enter.

"What's up, homie?" I reached for a super high five after placing my things down.

"What you got for me, Mrs. L?"

"First of all, you haven't even told me who I was shopping for, what her style is, or anything. All you said was size eight, and I'm supposed to work with that?" I laughed. Ken was one of my favorite clients. His personality was amazing, and he was always a pleasure to work with.

"I knew you would make it work, so I'm not worried." Ken took a seat on the white thinking chair in his living room.

"At least tell me if she's someone special," I said while pulling the clothes from the bags and laying them out on the sofa.

"Her name is Diamond, and she's very special." He was smiling that contagious smile of his. "I think she's the one, but I have to run her past Mom Dukes first, you feel me?"

"Oh, Lord, this must be serious then." In all the time Ken had been my client, I never saw him with a woman or even mention one for that matter. His head was so far into the game of basketball, people began speculating about his sexual preference.

"It is, and I need everything to go right, which is why I called you." Ken laughed. "I need baby girl to trade in those booty shorts for a nice sundress."

"Don't tell me she's a hot mama, Ken. Mama Tucker don't play that." I looked back at him while pulling out the shoes and accessories. I'd heard his mother was a beast and his sister was very protective of her little brother.

"Diamond has a little edge about her, which I love, but I don't want her to be misjudged by my family because of her attire." Ken looked down at the floor.

"How do you think Diamond will feel when she finds out you're trying to change her though?"

"I'm not trying to change her for good, just for the weekend." He laughed.

"I'm just saying love shouldn't come with limits. Your love life is none of my business, but if you love Diamond, you should love her flaws and all. What if she tried to change your wardrobe or told you to talk a certain way before you met her family? Would you like that?" I looked at Ken like a little brother. I didn't want him to lose someone who obviously made him happy for the sake of pleasing his mama.

"Damn, Lyric, now you got me feeling bad." Ken sat back in the seat while pondering my words.

"I'm not trying to do that, but you know I keep it one hundred. Beating around the bush isn't my thing." I shrugged with a smile.

"Speaking of which . . ." Ken cleared his throat. "Don't get mad at me for asking, but I saw an article about your company being in the red. Is that true, Lyric?"

Instantly, the air in the room became quite thick. I was mortified to have a client asking me about my financial report. My first reaction was to lie. "Of course not."

"Lyric." Ken eyed me suspiciously. "Come on, man. I thought me and you were better than that."

"Fine." I smacked my lips. "Yes, my company is in the red. If things don't turn around soon, I will have to close the doors of my business. It's nothing to be alarmed about right now. That's why I didn't say anything, but since you asked . . ." I felt defeated. For a very long time, I was able to keep my business personal from my friends, family, and clients. If Ken had read the article, there was no telling who else knew I was two steps away from the poverty line.

"Damn, Lyric, I was hoping that shit wasn't true." He sat back up in his seat. "What are you going to do?"

"I wish it weren't, Ken." I sighed. "Life happens, but I'll do everything I can to keep my doors open," I replied honestly.

"How much, Lyric?"

"I'm not here for a handout, Ken. Now that you know what I'm facing, I want you to obtain a backup stylist just in case." After setting up the clothing, I turned to face him.

"Look, I only want to work with you. We've been rocking since day one." He stood from his chair. "How much is your yearly retainer?"

"I charge forty thousand a year." Usually, a stylist had two options when taking on clients. The first was to be paid per event. The second option was to be paid in advance for the entire year. Basically, it meant you were on call at a discounted rate for every affair your client attended. Up until now, Ken was only a pay-per-event client.

"I got you."

"Ken, you don't have to do this." I didn't want him to see me as unprofessional for divulging my personal business as a way of swindling his money.

"Stop it." He walked away briefly before coming back with a check. "You're like family, Lyric. I'll never see your business in the red as long as I can help."

"This check is for eighty thousand dollars." My hand was trembling. "Ken," was all I could say before tears filled my eyes. I was totally overwhelmed by his kindness. "This is too much."

"That's for me and Diamond." Ken smiled. "I want you to style us both. She's going to be my wife real soon, and I have to make sure she's flawless at all times."

"Thank you so much. You really have no idea what this means." I was practically bawling like a baby. This boy had no idea that he had just paid my kids' tuition, put food in my refrigerator, and saved me from the repo man.

"Lyric, I know you're a good person with a great heart. In life, sometimes we encounter storms, but that doesn't mean God isn't still in the blessing business." Ken wrapped his arms around me, hugging me tightly.

I knew I was a mess and wanted badly to pull myself together. However, right now, I couldn't let go of my seven-foot savior. My ass was practically shouting about the blessing I'd just received as well as the word Ken had just delivered. It was confirmation that God was real and He would never see the righteous forsaken, even when we thought He was too busy to hear our cries.

Just then, the front door opened. In walked the infamous Diamond, looking like she was ready to throw punches.

# Chapter Eleven

## *Diamond*

"What the fuck is really going on around this bitch?" I asked my man and the little bitch he was all hugged up on.

"Diamond, this is my stylist, Lyric. I had her bring some pieces over for you," Ken replied nervously.

"Nigga, I'm grown as hell. I can pick out my own shit." Prepared for war, I set my purse down on the table. "Where I come from, bitches get killed for shit like this!"

"Diamond, I don't want your man." Homegirl sniffled and wiped her eyes. "I'm married to Damien Roberts." The skank said it like he was someone special.

"The crackhead?" I replied without remorse.

"Diamond!" Ken snapped. The bulging vein in his forehead indicated I had gone too far.

"Fuck you, bitch," shorty popped back at me before turning to my man. "Ken, I don't have to take this shit. Here's your money. I'm out."

"Lyric, don't go." Ken grabbed her arm. I didn't like the gesture, but I knew enough to keep my mouth closed. "Diamond, what the hell is wrong with you? This lady is a good friend of mine who came to do me a favor, and this is how you act."

"Baby, I'm sorry." I didn't like being in the doghouse with my man, so I tried to change my tune.

"Don't apologize to me. Apologize to Lyric," he scolded me like a child.

"I'm sorry, Lyric. I don't mean any harm. I'm just territorial about mine," I said grudgingly. "Think about it—I walk in and see a woman all hugged up with my man, and my mind went off the deep end." Casually, I walked over and wrapped my arms around my boo, creating distance between the two of them.

"I understand. It's all good." Lyric nodded.

I was sure she knew exactly where I was coming from.

"I can assure you there is nothing going on this way. Ken just retained me to style you for the year, so I hugged him to thank him for the business, that's all." Lyric smiled.

"Baby, you did?" I turned to Ken.

"I got to have my wifey looking her best at all times," Ken replied.

"Well, all right then." I turned back to Lyric. "Let me see what you picked out for his wifey." I walked over to the pieces laid out on the sofa.

"Well, I was only able to pull a few pieces because Ken called me last minute. He didn't give me much to work with other than your size. I hope you like it. If not, let's go back to the drawing board."

"Girl, this shit is deadly!" I squealed after looking over the ensembles Lyric had chosen without knowing me from a can of paint. "These Louboutins haven't even hit the runway yet."

"I have some good connections," Lyric said, then walked over to the clothes and started holding them up to my body. It felt good to be made a fuss over. I loved being the girlfriend of a wealthy nigga.

"Lyric is good people, Diamond. I want y'all to hang out from time to time. She could really show you the ins and outs of being a celebrity wife."

"Wife?" I was smiling so damn hard that all my teeth, cavities, and tonsils were showing.

"I would be happy to show her the ropes." Lyric nodded. "I think Diamond would make a great NBA wife."

"I love the sound of that," I squealed. "Uh, baby, don't you have a game to be getting to?" I looked up at Ken, who backed away with his hands up.

"I get the picture. I'll leave you guys to it."

"See you later," Lyric and I said in unison.

"Can you hook me up for the game tonight? I need to be fly."

"Absolutely. This is what I do," Lyric said before going to work on my outfit for the night.

When it was all said and done, homegirl had laced me with a black V-neck top with ruffles at the bottom and a denim pencil skirt and accessories. I felt sexy yet sophisticated.

"You'll fit right in with those basketball wives tonight." Lyric snapped her finger.

"Thank you, Lyric, and again, I'm sorry for coming at you like that." I was remorseful because I had totally misjudged her. She was a really cool person.

"No thank you needed, boo. Call me anytime you need something, and I got you." She began packing up her belongings.

"Ken is planning to have a get-together with his family sometime soon. Do you think we could meet up and go shopping before that so I can impress his mother?"

"Of course, Diamond." Lyric smiled.

"I really like him, and I know what his mother thinks about me will determine if I get the green light." As I spoke, I surprised myself with how open I was being with this stranger. However, Lyric was really down-to-earth, and we had a connection.

"Diamond, if I may drop some jewels on you, it would be to always remain yourself. I understand that you want to impress his mother, but don't change so much that you lose yourself in the process." With a smile, Lyric swung two garment bags across her shoulder and headed for the door.

I wanted to tell her there was so much dirt on my résumé that it wouldn't be a bad idea to lose my old self completely. I would've changed my whole identity if I could just escape my ratchet past. Had I known my path would lead me to this castle, living with my prince, I would've never kissed all those frogs in the first place.

Two hours later, I had shit, showered, and shaved. Right as I slid the towel dress over my head, the buzzer buzzed. Knowing it was my girl, Nisha, who was accompanying me to the game tonight, I buzzed her in without question. Seconds later, I heard the knock on the door and ran downstairs to unlock it. Because of the security gate and surveillance camera surrounding the condo, there was no peephole in the door. Therefore, I swung it wide open without a second thought. Standing there was Satan himself dressed in a red Dickie outfit and a St. Louis snapback with a toothpick dangling between his lips.

"Duck," I gasped, nearly jumping from my skin.

"A nigga had to come a long fucking way to find your ass." He smirked before stepping into the condo like he owned it.

"Why? How?" The words in my mind wouldn't form a proper sentence as I took in the ungodly sight before me.

Donald "Duck" Marshall was a skeleton I wished had stayed his ass in the fucking closet. Two years ago, he was my man and a big-time dope boy in Missouri. Duck was getting money faster than I could spend it, which was why I stayed with his ugly ass and endured all the shit he subjected me to. After being hit with both distribution and possession charges, Duck was sentenced to twelve years. The time apart provided a window of opportunity for me to do what I did best, which was to rob his ass blind. I stole everything he owned—money, jewelry, clothing, furniture, and cars. Then I sold everything on the black market. Temporarily, my pockets were swollen, but so was the lump in my throat the minute I got word that his ass had been set free sixty days later due to a "technicality." Using the last of my earnings from his shit, I hopped on the first plane to Los Angeles and never looked back. I thought being halfway across the country was far enough. However, by the looks of things, I should've gone a lot farther.

"What are you doing here?" I tried to calm my nerves.

"Diamond, you're too young to have Alzheimer's." He chuckled while checking out the condo. I watched as his eyes surveyed the expensive paintings on the wall, and my stomach turned. "You know exactly why I'm here."

"Look, Duck, I'm sorry about what happened back then. I was young and stupid." I followed him.

"Sorry? Oh, you will be sorry if I don't get my bread." He stopped abruptly, causing me to run into his back. Prison had done wonders for his body. The shit felt like a brick wall.

"I don't have any money," I pleaded.

"You must think I'm stupid." Duck turned to face me. "Bitch, I know whose house this is! You're fuckin' a millionaire, so getting my bread shouldn't be that hard." Duck waltzed over to the sofa and flopped down, putting his dirty shoes on the white furniture.

"Duck, me and him aren't like that. I mean, I can get a little dough, but not that much." I tried to calm my shaky hand.

"Diamond, I don't give a fuck if you have to rob this nigga like you did me or sell that stank-ass pussy." His stone-cold grimace had me shook. "I'll give you two weeks to put two million in my hand before you come up missing."

"Two million?" I almost fell over.

"Two million dollars in two weeks, or I will put two bullets right between your goddamn eyes." Duck made his fingers imitate a gun, then pulled the trigger.

# Chapter Twelve

## *Tionne*

The sound of the ringing phone on the nightstand stirred me from my slumber. "Hello."

"Mrs. Foster, this is the front desk. Sorry to disturb you but there is a problem with your credit card." The man on the other end cleared his throat.

"What kind of problem could there be with a black card?" I snapped. "It's limitless, so there shouldn't be anything wrong with it."

"Actually, it was declined, ma'am."

"Declined?" I sat up in the plush king-sized bed. "What?"

"It was declined. I'm sorry."

"There has to be some mistake!" I jumped from the bed as if it were on fire. "Try this one." I fumbled for my purse and retrieved an Amex. After reciting the fifteen-digit number, I waited.

"Unfortunately, this one is declined as well."

"Are you for real?" I shook my head and grabbed another card. Once again, I relayed the number, and once again, I was told the shit was declined. Finally fed up with this nonsense, I just told the guy to give me a second and I would be down with cash.

"Ain't this a bitch," I snapped while slipping on my pants and a pair of shoes. Without calling the card companies, I knew Dallas had cut me off. Lucky for me, I had enough cash on hand to cover a few nights at the W as well as a personal credit card that I applied for on my own.

With much attitude, I stormed down the hallway, stepped on the elevator, and headed to the front desk. Waiting for me was a tall white man with no facial hair. "Ah, Mrs. Foster." He smiled with recognition.

"I'm sorry about the cards. It appears my husband is playing dirty." I reached into my pocket and handed over the money. While the guy went about ringing me up, I glanced above his head where the television was. It was on E. They were covering the story on Joan Rivers, but on the bottom of the screen, I saw my name. I had missed the beginning of the crawl, but the end read, Tionne Foster was seen speeding away from the couple's Calabasas home in a rage. Sources say the couple is headed for splitsville again!

"Thank you, ma'am. Here is your receipt."

"Thanks." I took the paper, then headed back toward the elevator. In the lobby was a small convenience store. I stopped in to grab an orange and a pack of Tylenol to cure the headache that was assuredly lurking.

"Oh, my God, is that her?" I could hear from behind me.

"I think it is," someone else replied. As I approached the counter, they approached me.

"Excuse me, miss. Can you sign this please?" Some pimple-faced white girl with braces extended a tabloid my way. I looked down to see myself and Dallas on the cover with a squiggly line between us. Somehow, the owners of *Sloppy Gossip,* a popular tabloid magazine, had managed to get my story and print it in less than twenty-four hours.

"Little girl, you better get out of my face." Turning to face the counter, I tried to ignore the little bitch.

"I can see why Dallas is with a white woman instead of her." She giggled with her friend.

"I know, right." The friend laughed. "Black women have bad attitudes."

"First of all . . ." I turned to reply, but lucky for me, they had placed the magazine back on the rack and walked out.

"Don't let them get to you, girl." The cashier shook her head before handing me my items in a bag along with my change.

"Thanks." I grabbed my shit and quickly retreated to my room.

As soon as I entered, my cell phone started ringing. It was my girl Zuri. Although I wanted to talk to her, I let the call go to voicemail, then quickly dialed my house.

"Hello," some unfamiliar-sounding female answered while giggling.

"Who the fuck is this?" I barked.

"Who the fuck do you want it to be?" She laughed.

"Bitch, give Dallas the phone." I was beyond pissed off.

"Hello," Dallas answered as if it were perfectly normal to have another bitch in my house.

"Who the fuck was that, and why the fuck is she there?"

"That was Bridget, my new assistant."

"You fucking bastard! I haven't been gone long, and you already have a new bitch living up in my house?" Although crying was the last thing on my mind, I couldn't stop the tears from forming. I tried to act tough, but this shit was hurtful.

"Tionne, chill out with all of that. I ain't got nobody living here." Dallas laughed.

"You ain't shit but a dirty fucking dog, Dallas. One day you're going to end up with fleas." I was seething.

"You can kill that noise, all right? Besides, T, you left me, remember? When you walked out the fucking door, you gave me permission to do me. Don't get mad now."

"Fuck you, Dallas!"

"Tionne, is there a reason that you called in the first place?" Dallas sighed. "I have shit to do."

"You cut off my cards?"

"Actually, they weren't your cards in the first place. But yeah, I cut them off." The sound of Dallas's voice was sickening.

"Just last night you said you couldn't live without me. Today, you're being mean and vindictive. Your bipolar ass needs to see a fuckin' doctor."

"Well, I thought I couldn't live without you until you left. That's when I realized my house is still my house, my cars are still mine, my bills will be paid without you, and I'm still the fucking CEO of my own shit without you." Dallas started laughing hard.

"You see, Tionne, it's you who actually can't live without me. When you left here last night screaming that independent shit, you actually thought you was about that life, so I figured I would play along. I cut off the cards, closed the joint account, and I'll be turning your cell phone off shortly. Later today, someone will come and pick up the G-Wagen, since I know you're at the W." He snickered. "Tionne, if you want to be independent so bad, I want you to see what those independent bitches go through. The grass ain't always greener on the other side, ma."

"You're a fucking asshole."

"When you come to your senses, I'll be here waiting. Until then, remember to never bite the hand that feeds you."

# Chapter Thirteen

## *Jasmine*

Business ran as usual for the five days that King was home. The chef cooked. I cleaned the house and spent most of my time with Jordan. King, on the other hand, had a lot of running around to do. Sunday he slept all day. Therefore, we didn't make it to Stacey's party. On Monday, he played basketball with some of his old friends from high school, then hit the studio to record. Tuesday, he headed to one of the local after-school activity centers and talked with the kids. Wednesday was his busiest day because he took meetings with the label execs and reps from his clothing line to discuss the direction of his brand. Thursday was no fun either because he slept all day again. King barely acknowledged Jordan when he was home. It used to upset me. Unfortunately, over the past four years, I'd grown accustomed to it. Today was Friday, and we were in Los Angeles for the early screening of King's new movie, *Black in the Hood*. I didn't know what the movie was about. Nonetheless, I was really excited to see it on the big screen. My man was a movie star now, and I was very proud of him.

King was a bit antsy and on edge earlier at the hotel. He had snapped on the stylist and my makeup artist. For that reason, I stayed away from him until it was time to leave. I didn't need him being upset with me on such a beautiful day. As we rode down Hollywood Boulevard, I couldn't help but notice that King couldn't be still. He squirmed in his seat like a child who needed to use the potty.

"It's okay, baby. I know you did great." Recognizing that he was extremely nervous, I smiled reassuringly. We waited in line with the rest of the fleet of vehicles for about twenty minutes. During the entire time, a man walked alongside the SUV while speaking into a device on the cuff of his jacket.

"What is he doing?" I asked King.

"Oh, they do that so the camera crew and reporters can hear who's approaching. This shit is live on the air, so they need to be ready with questions," he explained as we finally made it to the front of the huge building.

"King James is in vehicle thirteen," the guy spoke into his cuff, then opened the door.

When we stepped from the black Escalade, cameras and microphones were instantly placed in our faces. "So, KJ, how does it feel to take a break from rapping and pursue an acting career?" a white reporter with a large nose asked.

"It feels awesome, you know. It's something I've always wanted to do, so I'm thankful I was given this opportunity." King flashed a smile and winked at the camera for good measure. He reached for my arm, and then we walked down the red carpet as more cameras flashed.

"KJ, what are you wearing tonight?" an Asian woman asked.

"This is Valentino." King opened his pinstriped suit jacket, did a slow spin, then posed for a quick picture.

"Thank you, KJ. Enjoy the premiere, and congrats on the movie," the reporter said as we walked into the lobby of the Belle Grand Hotel and Theater. People were everywhere, and I was excited. I had already spotted a few vets like Denzel and Angela. I tried to compose myself and not act like a groupie, but it was tough.

"Baby, should we go to our seats? The premiere starts in less than ten minutes." I glanced down at my Movado timepiece.

"Jasmine, do these people look like they're in a rush to you? Chill the fuck out," he snapped.

"Damn, King, I was just telling you so we won't miss anything," I said in my defense.

"Yeah, well, don't tell me anything else tonight, all right? All I need you to do is look pretty and be quiet." He released my arm, then walked toward the group of people I recognized as the movie's cast. I didn't know what to do, so I just stood there like a fool. I watched King smile for a few more pictures and drop a few more lines to reporters.

I scanned the room for a familiar face, but this scene was different from what I was accustomed to. At least at music industry events there was always a person I could talk to. Sometimes there were producers, DJs, or a few hip-hop wives. Other times, it was the singer or rapper themselves. Either way, I was in my element and felt at ease because I was in the "in" crowd. I could speak the lingo and knew all about the latest drama and gossip. This shit was too upscale. I felt out of place, like a party crasher. The room was packed with men in expensive suits and women in exquisite gowns, draped up and dripping with millions of dollars in jewelry. Soft music played in the background as waiters distributed champagne flutes and finger food. Small chatter and light laughter flowed throughout the room. I couldn't help but wonder how a person could feel so alone in a roomful of people.

Just as I was about to check my watch for the third time, I noticed a fine gentleman staring at me. "I'm sorry, am I in your way?" I asked since I was standing in front of the doors of the theater. All of the other people had walked around me. Therefore, I thought this guy was just trying to give me a hard time.

"No, beautiful, you're not in my way. Actually"—he pulled at his tie—"I was just coming over here to introduce myself. I'm Bradley Homes, and you are?"

I almost wet myself when he extended a hand and hit me with his Rembrandt smile. Mr. Homes was fine to say the least. He stood at least six feet, seven inches, with sun-kissed skin and short, dark, wavy hair. My guess was he was Hawaiian or something.

"Mr. Homes, my name is Jasmine, Jasmine James," I stuttered.

"Nice to meet you, Jasmine." He smiled again. "I saw you come in with King James. Is he your date?"

"No, well, yes, he is my husband." I needed to get it together and fast.

"Husband?" He sounded shocked. "I should've figured that since James is your last name too." He chuckled. "Anyway, I just wanted to come over and ask if you wouldn't mind passing him my card. I produce movies, and I have an upcoming role that I would love to cast him in. The guy's a natural. I would've given him the card myself, but I turned my back, and he disappeared on me. The movie is scheduled for production in two months. Maybe we could do lunch before he leaves California and talk about it." He looked back at the crowd, which was beginning to thin out, and I did the same.

"Yes, of course, Mr. Homes. I will definitely pass on the card along with your message to King, and lunch sounds great!" I reached for the card, then placed it inside of my red sequined Chanel clutch.

"Thanks, Mrs. James. If you'll excuse me, I've got to get going. My wife is waiting for me. She's ready to take our seats." He patted my shoulder and I smiled.

Time was ticking. We were about to miss the start of our premiere. I had already seen most of the cast members go inside the theater, all except King and that damn Melissa Valentine. I was about to reach for my cell phone when, out of nowhere, somebody snatched my wrist and yanked it.

"Bitch, are you serious? So you are just going to disrespect me like that?" It was King, looking deranged.

"What?" I asked while Melissa Valentine stood there snickering. "What the fuck are you talking about, King? And where in the hell have you been?" I wanted to know.

"Don't fucking question me. I'm the one who needs to be asking questions. Who the fuck was that Puerto Rican–looking nigga you was over here flirting with?" He squeezed my wrist tighter.

"Flirting? Wasn't nobody over here flirting. He came over here to—" I was cut off by King's voice.

"Over here to do what, bitch? I can't take your simple ass nowhere! All a nigga asked you to do was get dressed, look pretty, and shut the fuck up! You didn't need to start talking to nobody," he barked.

"Excuse me, sir, if you can't lower your voice and calm down, we're going to have to ask you to leave. The guests inside the theater are beginning to complain," a security guard explained to King.

"I ain't going no-fucking-where, bruh, so you need to back the hell up and let me handle my lady." King tried to brush the dude off, but it wasn't happening.

"Look, partner, I've warned you already. Next I'm going to have to call the police," the guard threatened.

"Well, my dude, you do what you have to," King shot back after letting my wrist go.

"King, calm down, baby. We don't need the police here." I tried reaching for his hand. I was ready to say, "Fuck the movie," and leave.

"Bitch, get yo' hood-rat ass away from me. I can't take you no-damn-where without you dick hopping over to the next nigga with money." He looked at me like he didn't even know who I was.

"Are you serious right now?" I screamed. People had begun to exit the movie theater and gather around us like we were the damn premiere.

"Yeah, you raggedy bitch. I made you, and this is how you do me? Where that nigga at?" He started searching through the crowd. I was beyond embarrassed. Putting my head down in shame, I attempted to walk away as quickly as possible.

"Bitch, you ain't going nowhere until I speak to that nigga. Where he at?" He pulled my hair and yanked me back.

"King, stop it! You're hurting me. Stop it please," I begged while the crowd of faces looked on.

"Hey, young brother, don't treat that beautiful sister like that," someone finally spoke out.

"Where is the nigga at, Jasmine?" He yanked again, causing me to trip on a snag in the carpet. One of my Jimmy Choos came off, causing me to hit the floor hard.

"King, stop it. Please, baby, stop," I cried as he dragged my ass. I tried my darndest to hold my dress down. Even so, I was sure my bare ass and shaved vagina were showing.

"Stop it? Am I embarrassing you, Jasmine? Well, you embarrassed me. You're my wife, and you over here flirting with a nigga at my event. How am I supposed to feel?" He stopped and looked down at me.

"King, the man came over to give me a business card," I said through tears. Since he was no longer dragging me, I quickly opened my clutch and produced the business card. "He wants you to take a role in his new movie. He couldn't find you, so he gave it to me." I stood and wobbled over to my other shoe. My entire body was in pain. All I wanted to do was bounce. My Indian weave was in disarray and flying all over the place. My sequined dress was ruined, the red, swollen rug burns on my thighs and arms looked hideous, my makeup was through, and I was mortified. Not only had King's tantrum been witnessed by a roomful of influential people, but it had also been recorded by the many cameras in the building.

"Ma'am, can I call somebody for you?" a young security guard asked as I walked away from the crowd.

"No, but is there a back way out of here?" I asked through tears.

# Chapter Fourteen

## *Zuri*

I leaned on the horn just as Tionne ran out into the rain. She had been waiting in the lobby of the hotel for me to pick her up and take her to her lawyer. She knew her car was safe in the hotel's parking garage and didn't want to run the risk of Dallas taking it if she left and had to park on the street.

"Thank you for coming to pick me up." Tionne reached over for a hug.

"Why the hell did I have to wait until you needed a ride for you to pick up the phone and call me?" I asked. "I thought we were tight." Tionne had been holed up at the W for over a week now, and I was annoyed that she hadn't answered my calls or dialed me sooner.

"Girl, you know it ain't like that. I just needed some time, you know." Tionne sighed.

"Bitch, I got all the time in the world. I would've come over and cried with you, yelled with you, and kicked that motherfucker's door in if need be." My joke was to lighten the mood, but Tionne merely stared out the window. "It's going to be all right." I patted her thigh.

"Is it, Z? I mean, I just can't believe that bastard threatened to steal my fucking car. Who does that?"

"A lame-ass nigga, that's who." I laughed, and this time Tionne did too. "Seriously, he calls himself breaking you down so you'll come crawling back, but fuck him. I got you, bitch!" I reached for a high five.

"I know you do, Z." Tionne slapped her palm into mine, and we shared a brief moment of silence.

She and I had been best friends going on ten years now. We met at a fashion show during New York Fashion Week. Tionne had been invited as the guest of the designer, and I, of course, was one of the models. The show was such a success that the designer decided to treat a few of his models and friends to dinner and drinks. As luck would have it, Tionne was seated next to me. We hit it off instantly and had been trump tight ever since. In a world full of fake friends and false admirers, Tionne was my ace. There was nothing in the world I wouldn't do for her and vice versa.

"Thanks, Z. I really owe you one." Tionne reclined in the seat.

"Girl, I know if the shoe were on the other foot, you would have me too." I released the brake and put the SUV in motion.

"That's what friends are for, although your ass has the perfect marriage and won't ever need me." She smiled. "Jason is the shit!"

"I guess." I shrugged. Tionne was my bestie, but some things needed to remain between husband and wife. Therefore, I never told her about the abuse.

"I wish Dallas were more like Jason—faithful, loving, giving, and finneeeee," she exclaimed. I wanted to tell her to be careful what she wished for, but instead I concentrated on the road.

During the ride, no one said a word. Therefore, Tionne decided to break the silence. "Aren't you going to ask me why I left this time?"

"No, I wasn't," I said without looking at her. This wasn't my first rodeo with Tionne and Dallas. I was sure it wasn't going to be my last. As a result, I learned long ago not to ask questions.

"Why not?"

"Because, T, it doesn't matter." I sighed. "Look, don't take this the wrong way, but I know the way this is going to play out already. This is not the first time you've called me to come and get you, and I'm sure this won't be the last." Although Tionne was used to my bluntness, I could tell she was still taken aback by my words. "Tionne, I didn't mean to hurt your feelings," I said, trying to clean it up.

"This time is different, I swear," Tionne mumbled. Based on her previous actions, she realized it was difficult to believe her. I knew she wanted me to.

"What makes this different from the last time you caught his ass butt naked at the studio? What about the time that bitch showed up on your doorstep? No, I've got one better." I laughed, unaware of my friend's tears. "What about the time he had a threesome with those two sisters and both of their asses claimed he was the father of their children?" I could go on for days. Dallas was a wild card for sure.

"He burned me," Tionne cried. I almost wrecked the car, barely missing a pedestrian as I ran the red light.

"He did what?"

"He gave me chlamydia," Tionne admitted sadly.

"Oh, girl, you scared me. I thought you had something much worse." I breathed a sigh of relief. The thought of my best friend being taken out of the world by her no-good husband really shook me up. "I'm sorry, Tionne. Are you okay?"

"I'm good now. The doctor gave me a prescription last week." She wiped her eyes. "I know I've said over and over I was leaving, but this time is different, I swear. There was something about the doctor's office calling to tell me that my results came back positive for something and to get in the office as soon as possible that shook me up." Tionne looked out of the window. "What if it had been AIDS?"

"Thank God it's not." I patted her shoulder. I could only imagine how Tionne was feeling.

"It was a wakeup call for me though. If that bastard wants to play Russian roulette with his life, that's his business. I won't let him kill me in the process."

"Well, for your sake, I hope if ever the day comes that he persuades you to go home, you remember this day and those words."

"You don't have to worry. I'm done with Dallas Foster aka Black Bishop and all the bullshit that comes with both of those motherfuckers." Tionne shook her head.

I was certain she never imagined marrying a celebrity came with so much drama. None of us did. I was sure people tried to warn her, but she was blinded by young love.

"Good thing you don't have any children. It makes the breakup easier," I said, thinking of my own situation. If ever I found the strength to leave Jason, Jelly would be the one to suffer. "I can't imagine having to share my baby between two homes on weekends, summer vacations, and holidays."

"I'm ready to just start over with my life, Z. God is giving me a second chance, and I want to run with it."

"Where do you go from here?" I asked. "What's your plan B?" From what I knew about Tionne, she didn't have any education beyond high school and had never held a job.

"I don't know. I was thinking about starting an interior design company, but it depends on what my lawyer says today. Hopefully, I'll get enough in the divorce settlement for start-up money."

"That's a good idea." My girl was a beast when it came to decorating. Her home was proof of that. She had even done Jelly's nursery last year as a gift and a thank-you for us choosing her as the godmother.

"In order for it to be successful, I'll have to take some business classes and drum up some clientele," she began to ramble.

"Running a business is hard work, but I know you'll do great."

"Hopefully, I can get enough start-up money though. If I can't, then I don't know what I'll do." Tionne looked worried.

"Everything will be all right. I know you'll get more than enough money in the settlement, T."

"I signed a prenup," Tionne blurted out before looking down at the floor.

"What!"

"I know, I know."

"Maybe there's a loophole or something." I wanted to stop the car and ask her what the hell she was thinking, but now wasn't the time.

"I hope so." Tionne smacked her lips. "I thought we would be together forever. So it didn't seem right to plan my divorce before we planned our wedding."

Nearly an hour later, we made it through rush hour traffic and arrived at the law office of Marsha Whitehead, attorney at law. The place was gigantic with oversized furniture, hardwood floors, chandeliers, and oil paintings. It stood four stories tall!

"Mrs. Whitehead will see you now," the receptionist announced after approaching us in the second-floor lobby.

As we followed her, I eyed Tionne closely. She was a nervous wreck. "It'll be okay, T." I grabbed her hand and held on to it tightly.

"Ladies, come on in and have a seat," Marsha greeted us from her chair.

"Thanks for meeting with me on such short notice." Tionne reached over to shake her lawyer's hand.

"Anything for you, Mrs. Foster." Marsha grabbed a few documents from a folder. "Let's get straight to it, okay?" She waited for Tionne to agree before continuing. "Okay, I read over the prenuptial agreement you signed before marrying Mr. Foster. My findings were rather shocking if I may." She pushed the black frames up onto her nose. "Without going word for word, the summary of this document states that you are entitled to absolutely nothing."

"What about the house?" I interjected.

"Mrs. Foster did not put her name on the deed." Marsha looked down at the paperwork. "Nor did she sign off on the luxury vehicles, vacation properties, yacht, or jet. Furthermore, she is not included as a partner in Mr. Foster's business."

"So there isn't any mention of spousal support or anything?" I had to speak up for Tionne, who was silent.

"Spousal support would have only been granted if Mrs. Foster had given Mr. Foster a child." Marsha removed her glasses.

"So I get nothing? Absolutely nothing?" Tionne shook her head. "I'm the one who helped build his empire brick by brick. It was my goddamn blood, sweat, and tears." She hit the corner of Marsha's desk in a rage.

"Tionne, did you at least put something up for a rainy day?" I asked.

"No," she mumbled as the realization of her situation hit her like a brick wall. Marsha looked at me, and I looked at my friend. Both of us had encountered many women like Tionne, who were so busy living the glamorous life that they forgot that fairy tales weren't real.

# Chapter Fifteen

## *Diamond*

Seeing Duck the other night had me shook. Everywhere I went I couldn't help but feel as if he were following and watching me. It had gotten so bad that I barely left the house. All I wanted to do was lie up under Ken. I realized that I needed to put a plan in motion ASAP. Duck was serious about his $2 million, which was why I was scared shitless. Back in the day, I'd known him to body many people. Therefore, killing me wouldn't be a problem, which was why I put on my game face and did what I did best—grind by any means necessary.

"Lick my ass, Diamond," Stewart McKinnon begged with his legs spread-eagle up in the air. Instantly, my heart dropped down to my stomach.

"Don't you like this head, daddy?" I continued licking all around his wrinkled balls in disgust. His penis was so small that it wouldn't stay in my mouth, which was why his sack got all of the attention.

"I haven't had it licked in a while," Stewart begged. He was an old television producer with paper. We used to trick a while back whenever his wife was out of town. Stewart normally had odd requests, but this was, by far, the most ridiculous of them all.

"I don't lick ass."

"But I'm in need, Diamond."

"What's it worth to you?" With my index finger, I traced small circles around his anus in an attempt to tease him. Watching him get excited had me about to throw up.

"How much more do you want?" He looked down at me.

"Give me another three grand, and I'll lick your asshole dry." I sounded more excited than I actually was. Ass licking wasn't something I enjoyed at all, but it did bring in the money.

"Damn it. You want three grand on top of the five I just gave you?"

"You know how this works. Give me what I want, and you'll get what you need." I made a show of licking my elongated tongue around my lips.

"Shit," he gushed. "Deal!" Stewart spread his legs so far back that I heard his thigh bones crack.

Closing my eyes, I extended my tongue and dug into the brown hole below his nut sack. Inside was moist, warm, and very loose, which meant Stewart had received more than a tongue up his duke chute. The mere thought of his old ass having bisexual activity repulsed me.

"Damn, I missed you, Diamond." Stewart was in la-la land after only five minutes of ecstasy.

"I missed you too," I said while pulling my tongue out of his ass and putting it back into my mouth. The taste of some kind of cream was left behind, so I casually grabbed a throw pillow from the bed and ran my tongue across it. Stewart slowly brought his legs down and went to retrieve his trousers lying across the footboard. Leisurely, he pulled out a few bills and placed them in my hand.

"I added another five hundred just because you were a good sport about it." Stewart handed me the money before slipping on his pants. "I take it you remember the way out, right?"

"Yes, I remember. See you next time." I nodded and grabbed my purse. On my way out of the bedroom, I caught a glimpse of a tube of Preparation H on the nightstand, which meant the creamy residue I tasted was the ass ointment. It took everything in me not to cuss his trifling ass out. Instead, I decided to get even.

Once downstairs, I took my time about letting myself out because I knew the place was empty. Going from room to room, I searched for anything of value that I could sell in the streets. Stewart was in his seventies, so most of his belongings were old. However, a quick rummage in the kitchen uncovered several fourteen-karat gold plates, saucers, and cups. Swiftly, I grabbed as many as I could, then made a beeline for the door. I was pretty sure I looked like a fool running down the street toward my whip with my arms full of dishes. Even so, if I took them to the hood, I knew I could flip them for a small profit. At this point, something was better than nothing. I needed all I could get before Duck came looking for his dough.

I hit the lock on the red BMW and watched the trunk rise. Hastily, I unloaded my stolen items, then prepared to hop in and take off. But as soon as I closed the trunk, I was scared shitless.

"Still up to your old tricks, I see."

"Duck, you've got to stop popping up like that for real." I grabbed my heart.

"Just checking up on you to see about my bread, that's all." He smirked.

"Nigga, you gave me two weeks, remember?" I smacked my lips and pushed past him.

"Oh, I remember, but you best not forget." Duck lifted his navy Polo shirt to reveal a large-caliber gun tucked into the waistband of his jeans.

My stomach did a backflip. There was no doubt that if I didn't come through with the money, my ass would end up in a ditch.

The sound of my phone caused him and me both to look down at my purse. With both eyes on Duck, I reached down and grabbed it. "Hello. Hey, baby." Shit, it was Ken. "Uh, I'm just leaving the mall."

"Get my fucking money, Diamond, or else." Duck backed away after patting his stomach. I watched as he hustled over to the waiting Ford Mustang and drove off.

"Who was that?" Ken asked.

"Nobody, baby. I miss you." I tried to play it cool while stepping into my ride and starting the engine. "I hate that your game is away tonight, but I'll be watching, boo."

"I know you're my number one cheerleader," Ken spoke over the chatter of his loud-ass teammates. "Look, baby, I have to go, but I wanted to tell you that Mom Dukes is having a big birthday party back home in Alabama next week. I want you to get with Lyric and go shopping. It's going to be a big weekend."

"Okay, I'll call her tomorrow. Have a good game." Hitting the end button on the screen, I rested my head on the headrest for a second. The thought of going to Alabama scared the shit out of me for two reasons. Foremost, I wasn't thrilled at all about meeting "Mom Dukes." Second, I needed all the time I could get to obtain Duck's loot. Although it was only for a weekend, that was too long to be off my hustle.

Just as I opened my eyes, I saw Stewart emerge from his house. His head swiveled from side to side like he was searching for someone. I knew he couldn't have missed the dishes yet, but that didn't stop me from getting the fuck out of dodge.

About an hour later, I pulled up in East Hollywood, a sketchy part of Tinseltown. There were hood niggas and Latinos on just about every other corner. Prostitutes strutted like peacocks along with the occasional home-less person on a stroll with a buggy full of shit.

"Damn, Diamond, where you been?" Li'l Sonto nodded from the curb. He was the 11-year-old son of my friend Grace, although his ass acted like he was 22.

"Sonto, you better watch your mouth, boy." I smiled before popping the trunk and grabbing the goods. Grace was the number one booster on her side of town. If you wanted to buy anything, you called Grace, and if you wanted to sell anything, you called Grace.

"I don't believe my eyes." Grace stepped from behind the wrought iron gate on her front door wearing coochie cutters, fishnet stockings, knee boots, and a black button-down shirt. People in California dressed weird to me. "Bitch gets with a ball player and forget about her people," Grace shouted to no one in particular.

"Never that. I've just been busy." I leaned in to kiss her cheek since my arms were too full for a hug.

"Miss me with that bullshit." Grace reached into her pocket to retrieve a pack of cigarettes. "Nah, I'm just fucking with you. You know you're my girl." She lit the cigarette before taking some of the dishes from my hand and looking them over. "Nice."

"I need top dollar. What you think you can get for them?" I watched her inspect the plates like she was a genuine appraiser.

"They're good and heavy." She turned them on the back. "Fourteen karats I see."

"You know I wouldn't bring you no average dishes." I laughed.

"I'll give you two grand for the whole set."

"Deal." Two grand sounded like music to my ears. I didn't even try to wheel and deal.

"Come on in." Grace headed back into her run-down home with me following suit.

Once inside, I set my load down on the coffee table and took a seat on the torn pleather sofa. The place needed to be cleaned severely. There were food containers, pop bottles, glasses, and several ashtrays cluttering up the joint among other things. "Don't mind the mess." Grace made a show of trying to get some laundry off the sofa.

"Girl, I know your house is the party house." I laughed. Grace's place was a revolving door for some of Los Angeles's most treacherous residents. I loved my girl, but I would never be caught dead over here after dark.

"Let me grab your money, and then we can catch up." With an armful of clothing, she retreated toward the back of the house.

While she was gone, I noticed several pictures on the mantel above the fireplace. My eyes scanned each one until they rested on a food scale with a Ziploc bag full of vials. Curiosity pulled me from my seat to get a closer look. My brother had been in the dope game for so long that I knew the vials were filled with heroin, the most deadly and addictive drug on the market. "Goddamn," I mumbled. The bag had to be filled with over one hundred vials. Performing a quick tabulation in my head, I knew there was at least $20,000 sitting here, begging me to take it.

"This dumb-ass safe is acting up again, Diamond. Give me a minute," Grace called from the back room.

"Take your time, girl," I yelled back before grabbing the Ziploc and pouring a few vials into my purse.

"Grace, what you got to eat? I'm starving." A large Hispanic man burst through the front door, completely catching me off guard. Instinctively, I forced the whole bag of heroin into my purse and took a seat. There was no way for me to put the shit back now.

"Your big ass is always looking for food. You need to be running from the dinner table." Grace walked back into the living room with a smile. "Diamond, this is my boo, Neho. Neho, this is my girl Diamond, the one I was telling you about."

"What's up." He nodded, then started toward the kitchen.

"Don't mind him, girl. He's much friendlier once he eats." With a laugh, she handed over the money.

"Thanks, Grace." I folded the bills, then stuck them in my back pocket. After all, there was no way I could open my purse in front of her.

"So tell me what it's like." Grace flopped down beside me.

"What's what like?"

"Being a celebrity's wife."

"Well, I'm not a wife yet, but it's cool for the most part." I shrugged. Grace and I once swung from the same pole. It felt weird to be bragging about how my life turned out for the better when she was still in the same situation.

"Maybe one day I'll meet my prince and he'll whisk me away from the ghetto too." She looked back at Neho, who wasn't paying us any attention.

"It'll happen, Grace. If I find another prince, I'll send him your way." I winked.

"Well, until then, I'll be here selling dogs, dishes, and dope, or whatever I can just to feed my son." Grace laughed, but I knew she was serious. "Nah, but for real, I'm happy for you, Diamond." She reached over to hug me.

Instantly, I felt bad. The heroin I'd just stolen was ultimately taking food from Sonto's mouth.

"Thanks, girl." I stood and grabbed my purse. "Next time you come out to my neck of the woods we'll hang for the day, okay?" To be honest, I had no plans of seeing Grace or anyone from my past life ever again.

"Why are you leaving? You just got here."

"I promised to meet Ken for dinner." Truth was the sun was going down, which meant it was time to get the fuck back to my side of town.

# Chapter Sixteen

## *Jasmine*

It had been twenty-four hours, and I was still raging. "How could he? I mean, it was one thing to accuse me of cheating, but it was another thing to do it in a roomful of people while pulling my hair," I screamed into my phone.

"Wait until this nigga gets back in the D. I got heat for niggas like that," Stacey yelled.

"I swear, I'm done with this shit. I can't take it anymore, Stace. The killing part is the whole time the nigga was in my face yelling, his breath was smelling like pussy! He fucked the bitch and ate her pussy while my dumb ass waited in the lobby." I shook my head and wiped at a tear. I was dressed in a peach Juicy Couture sweatsuit with gold sandals, gold hoop earrings, and my real hair slicked back into a ponytail. After leaving that nightmare of an event yesterday, I checked into a Holiday Inn that was about eight miles away from our room at the W. I paid the concierge to transport my luggage over here and begged her not to tell King where I was. I took a long shower, washed my hair, and removed my tracks. I turned off my cell phone and refused to watch television or turn on the radio. I knew that it wouldn't take long for my business to hit the airwaves, so I needed time to reflect before it did.

My only reason for turning my phone on today was to check in with my mom and Jordan, then book a flight home. The minute my signal came in, my shit began to blow up. There were fifty messages, most of which were not from King. They were from his publicist, Danielle, my mom, and a few other relatives, who had more than likely seen that crazy shit on *TMZ* or something.

"Do you want me to come out there?" Stacey asked, grabbing my attention.

"No, I'm cool. I'm leaving here first thing in the morning. Tonight I'm just going to chill here at the hotel. I might call Amelia to see if she's available for dinner," I said, thinking about my good friend who lived in Cali. Amelia was the ex-girlfriend of Kold Hart, another rapper in the game. She left his ass last year after finding out he had gotten two people pregnant during their relationship. Since then, she'd made a name for herself in the fashion industry both as a model and designer.

"Okay, that's cool. Well, tell Amelia hello for me, and I'll see you tomorrow."

We ended the call, and then I walked onto the balcony to catch some sun. It was beautiful outside. It felt good to have some alone time. No King, no press, no Jordan, no anything. I didn't have to be a mom, wife, nurse, teacher, and maid all while in six-inch heels and smiling for the cameras. Actually, it felt good to be makeup free with no hair extensions. This reminded me of the old days. I was enjoying this time away from my real life.

I sat down on the tan lounge chair, put on my Dolce & Gabbana shades, then dialed my mother.

"Hello."

"Hey, Mama. How are you and Jordan?" I asked.

"Hey yourself, baby girl. We're good, but how are you, baby?" I could tell by the tone in her voice that she already knew what was up.

"So you've heard, huh?"

"Yes, baby, it's all over the place. What happened? What did you do to make him that mad?" she said out of concern.

I stopped and stared at the phone in disbelief. "Mama, why would you think it was me?" I asked, bewildered. My mama had always had my back. There must've been a good reason for her to ask what I had done.

"Well . . ." She let her word hang in the air.

"Well nothing, Mama. I didn't do anything to him. He ran off to go fuck some actress and left me in the lobby of the hotel. A man came up to me with a business card for King. He said he wanted to cast him in his next movie, so I put the card in my purse. The man walked away. King walked up and went ape shit on me, pulling my hair and dragging me." I waited for her to speak.

"Jasmine, are you sure that's what happened?"

"Am I sure? I know you didn't ask me if I am sure. I was there, and so were about a thousand other people. Go ask them." I was beyond pissed and about to hang the phone up.

"Calm down, honey. I only asked because the report that I watched didn't mention anything about him putting his hands on you. It said that you had too much to drink and openly flirted with some man at the premiere. It also said that King was really embarrassed because you were sloppy and falling all over the place." She paused and cleared her throat. "Baby, they even showed pictures of you on the floor trying to cover your private parts."

I gasped at what she was saying. "I swear on my son that was not what went down. This is all Danielle's doing. That bitch," I spat. "Look, Mama, I have to go. Kiss my son and tell him I'll be there tomorrow." I tapped the end button on my phone screen, then immediately dialed Danielle.

"Danielle Crawford," she answered on the second ring.

"Bitch, why in the fuck would you spin the story like that? You know that's not what happened," I yelled.

"Excuse me, but I'm no one's bitch." She cut into me. "First of all, Mrs. James, let me remind you that I don't work for you. I work for Mr. James. My best interest lies with him," she said as a matter of fact.

"You're dirty, Danielle. You know what he did to me, yet you sold me out. Protecting him only makes him think it's okay to do the things he does, and you're foul for that." I was about to cry because I was hurt.

"Jasmine, let me tell you something. Protecting him only means I get paid and so do you. If King gets locked up or looks like the bad guy in the press, no one eats. Do you understand that?" She attempted to scold me like a child. "So what? We had to make it look like you were the one out of pocket. So what? We had to pay people to back up our story, and so fucking what your feelings are hurt? At the end of the day, we averted a disaster that could've ended King's career. You have to learn that taking one for the team will happen every once in a while. You have to do your part and play your position if it keeps food on the table, clothes on your back—designer clothes, I might add—and pays for your son's medical bills," she ranted.

"Don't say anything about Jordan," I screamed as the tears rolled down my face.

Danielle sighed. "Jasmine, off the record, King is the biggest asshole I know. Do I condone the shit that he does to you? No, I don't. But it's a job, and I do it well because it pays my bills. Am I sorry that this happened to you? Yes, I am. However, you stay and continue to except his bullshit time after time. You're a beautiful young woman with so much to offer this world. I think it's time for you to do you and leave his ass. Then again, if I know you like I believe I do, your ass isn't going anywhere." Her words hit me like a ton of bricks. "Now if you don't mind, Jasmine, I have to take another call. I'll speak with you later. Goodbye."

# Chapter Seventeen

## *Lyric*

Within the week, I had received two blessings. The first one came from Ken, and the second came from Damien. He secured the role in the movie he auditioned for and was waiting for them to start production. The leading role came with the wage of $150,000, but due to his track record, he had to wait until the movie wrapped before he would see a dime of his earnings. Therefore, your girl was back on the move trying to find new ways to rob Peter to pay Paul.

"You know, Lyric, you would be great for this show I'm doing." China, my client, looked down at me as I pinned the hem on her skirt. She was the girlfriend of Young Guap, a Southern rapper new on the scene.

"What show?" I asked without really wanting to know. There was so much shit on my mind that whatever she was saying sounded like Morse code.

"*Celebs and the Women Who Love Them*," she stated nonchalantly.

"Oh, is it new? I've never heard of that one." After finishing the hem, I grabbed the portable steamer and went about tackling the wrinkles in her blouse.

"Girl, it's only the hottest franchise in the history of reality TV. Where have you been?"

"Apparently under a rock." I laughed. "I'm always working, so I never get to watch television."

"That's why you should do the show for your company. The cameras follow you around almost all day. You could show the world that some celebrity wives actually do work, while at the same time promoting your shit." China seemed to have it all figured out. "Not to mention getting that reality check." She rubbed her stiletto nails together.

"If you don't mind me asking, how much are those checks?" Now that we were talking money, she had my attention.

"Everybody is paid a different amount, but they start you off at fifty Gs. The more you bring to the table, the more money you make. Hell, I plan on being the biggest bitch on the network."

"Straight up?"

"Yeah, girl." She smacked her lips.

"I don't think I could act a fool on national television." I could just imagine my mother cringing.

"Fuck all that. I'm trying to get paid. I don't care nothing about what people think." She laughed before slipping into the McQueens resting before her. "Some of those bitches clear at least a quarter million or better."

"Really?"

"Girl, you need to get on this train before it pulls off." China made train noises with her mouth.

"What's the producer's number?" I knew China had probably trumped up the pay scale, but it was still worth making the call. Who could pass up a paycheck and free publicity?

"No need to call her. She should be arriving any minute. Today they're shooting my scenes. That's why I needed you to style me. I can't be on TV looking busted," she said just as the doorbell rang. While she went to answer her door, I started packing up my things.

As I pondered my future in television, a barrage of people swarmed the place with lighting and cameras. "Move that atrocious sofa now, and put the fucking cat up," a lady yelled from behind the biggest pair of sunglasses I'd ever seen. "I hate cats."

"Sorry, Linda. I didn't know," China apologized.

"Now you do, so please don't let it happen again." Linda removed the sunglasses from her face, then placed them on top of her head. "Who are you?" She stared me up and down.

"Linda, this is my friend Lyric. She's a stylist. We thought she may be a good fit for the show. Lyric, this is Linda Schmidt, the genius behind the *CATWWLT* craze."

"What is *CATWWLT*?" I hated to be rude, but I didn't know what in the world that meant.

"*Celebs and the Women Who Love Them*," China whispered. Almost everyone in the room gasped like I was supposed to know. "Lyric is a virgin to all of this, which is why she would be perfect." China laughed.

"I see." Linda continued to stare me down. "You have five minutes to brief me on why you want a spot on my show, starting now." She snapped her fingers, and I rolled my eyes.

"First off, who said I wanted a spot on your show?" I didn't like her attitude.

"What Lyric meant to say was she's not only a celebrity wife, but she's a mom and a mogul. She wants to share the ins and outs of her life with the world," China added. If the girl wasn't trying to be the next big reality bitch, she could've definitely had a job in PR.

"Boring," Linda barked. "I'm already over it." She yawned.

"Fuck it then," I barked back. I was already tired of her dramatics.

"Her husband is Damien Robertson," China shouted as a last-ditch effort to secure my spot on the show. Immediately, Linda's eyes rose, and a smile that resembled the Grinch's took over the frown she once possessed.

"Damien Robertson, as in the Damien Robertson who ran through LAX butt naked a few months ago?" Linda recalled a situation I wished I could forget. During one of his drug binges, my husband showed up at the airport high and acting erratic. Police tried to detain him, but he evaded them. While running, Damien thought it was a good idea to strip down to his birthday suit. He was later arrested for public indecency. "Mrs. Robertson, I would love to have you aboard." She extended a hand my way.

Quite naturally, I hesitated before reciprocating the gesture.

"Linda, I want some time to think before I sign on." I really needed to talk things over with Damien before making a decision. I also had to think about how this could potentially affect my children.

"The spot won't be open for long, Mrs. Robertson," Linda threatened, like that would make me sign up any sooner.

"Look, lady, I'm not one of these little girls around here begging for a chance at fame and fortune. I've been there, done that, and written the fucking book about it. I don't need no D-list celebrity status. I've been walking on red carpets since you were probably somebody's intern. Google me, bitch." With those words, I grabbed my shit, then headed for the door.

On the way to my car, I made a mental note to call China later and apologize. I really didn't mean to offend her with my jabs, especially when she was trying to help me out.

"Lyric, wait up," China called from her door.

"I'm sorry about all that." I walked up to her as she struggled not to scuff her borrowed McQueens running down the driveway.

"Girl, forget all of that. Linda just grabbed her checkbook and told me to give you this." She flashed a $300,000 check in my face. "I didn't even get that much!"

"As sexy as it looks, I can't take it."

"Why not?" China frowned.

"I'm just not with this." I shook my head. Money was the root of evil, and I wasn't down with making deals with the devil.

"Just take it, and I'll tell her you'll think about it." China forced the check into my hand before turning to head back into the spotlight.

# Chapter Eighteen

## *Jasmine*

Four hours after I spoke with Danielle, her words were still heavy on my mind. I replayed the conversation over and over until there was a knock at my room door. I looked at my watch. My girl Amelia was right on time.

"Here I come, girl," I called out as I grabbed my Dooney & Bourke hobo bag off the cream sofa. We had plans for dinner and taking in the newest Tyler Perry movie.

"What's up, diva," Amelia shouted from the door as I opened it. My girl was fierce in a denim halter top and matching capris. Her makeup was flawless, and her body was in great shape. As a matter of fact, I'd never seen Amelia look so good. I didn't know if it was the new blond hair or the peaceful look on her face, but my girl looked great. She was standing there with a bag of carryout that smelled delicious in her right hand and her custom LV bag along with a movie rental bag in the left.

"Girl, you must've sensed that I wasn't really feeling the crowds." I took the carryout bag from her and let her pass.

"Yeah, girl, I've been there, and I definitely understand." She put the movie bag down, then embraced me with a warm hug. It felt really good to have a friend right now, especially since Stacey was back in the D.

"Did you see that shit on the blogs? They got your girl looking bad." I tried to laugh it off.

"Girl, you know I ain't no blog reader, but my girl Tina was at the premiere. She told me the real deal. She said after Danielle and her team got through with the place, nobody could recall what had actually happened. All the A- and B-list celebrities didn't give a fuck. The C- and D-list celebrities were just happy to be invited to the premiere. Child, and the fans were all too geeked to do what Danielle asked as long as they got a KJ autograph and twenty-five dollars in gas money." Amelia cracked up laughing, and I did too.

"Girl, I didn't know fame would be like this. I thought me and King would be different, you know. Back in Detroit, when we were broke nobodies, we had each other's backs. I thought it would be the same way once we came up out the hood," I said, popping the lid on the Thai containers. My girl had hooked me up with my favorite: pad thai with broccoli, the number twenty sauce, and two egg rolls with extra house sauce for dipping.

"Like Biggie said, 'Mo' Money Mo' Problems.' These niggas get money, and they forget who had their backs when they didn't have a pot to piss in or a window to throw it out of." She grabbed her food and sat down Indian style on the floor by the couch. There was a dinette set right there, but I guessed she wanted to go old school, so I plopped down and joined her.

"I know that's right. I'm just tired of pretending. I'm so over this lifestyle it's not even funny." I took a bite of my egg roll. "Fuck the house, the money, the cars, fame, and fuck King too," I snapped.

"You sound like me when I left Gordon. I'm sorry, I mean, 'Kold Hart.'" She made air quotes. "He had been my man for nine years. All I wanted was a ring and a baby, but he didn't want to give me either. Then out of nowhere while we were in bed watching the Kardashians, an alert scrolled across the bottom of the screen. It read that congratulations were in order to the D.C. rapper Kold Hart and his longtime girlfriend, Shaniya, on the birth of their daughter. It also reported it was the rapper and model's second child." She rolled her eyes.

"Oh, my God, girl! What did you do?" I asked with a mouthful of noodles.

"I didn't say shit that night, but the next day he left to do a video shoot, and my ass called all my girls. Within eight hours, I had purchased a new condo and moved my shit out of his house and into my own. I also deposited two million dollars into my bank account from his." She laughed. "Child, just as that nigga was pulling into the gate, me and five of my friends were riding out of the gate, waving and blowing the horns on all his motherfucking cars. Trina was in the Land Rover, Jessie was in the Lamborghini, Daisha was pushing the Rolls-Royce, Vicky was in the Phantom, Toni was in the Mercedes, and I flexed hard in the Maybach." As she spoke, we slapped fives, and I laughed hysterically.

"Bitch, you got balls. I wish I were like that." I lay back on the floor and daydreamed.

"Just wait until you've had enough. You might be surprised at what you'll do." Amelia lay down beside me. She must've been full, because she loosened her Hermès belt and undid the top button on her capris. The girl was a solid size two, but she ate like a man.

"I told you I'm done with him. When I get home, I'm moving out, and I mean that." I looked over at her, and she rolled her eyes.

"Child, you aren't at your breaking point yet." She shook her head.

"How do you know?" I questioned.

"Because if you were, we wouldn't be here eating Thai and talking shit! Your ass would've been on the first thing smoking back to Detroit. You would've been on the phone with lawyers and a real estate agent, not lounging around with me like life is beautiful." She put her hand over mine. "But, Jasmine, that's okay. Like I said, you'll know when you've had enough because you'll end up surprising yourself." She winked.

The rest of the evening went swell. We watched *Diary of a Mad Black Woman* and *Waiting to Exhale*. I guessed Amelia was dropping hints. About an hour after she left, I was about to get into the tub. With a five a.m. flight, I needed to retire early tonight.

As soon as my big toe touched the scalding hot water, there was a knock at the door. *Of course!* I wrapped up in the hotel's plush white robe and headed for the door. I glanced around the room to see if Amelia had forgotten anything. "Who is it?" I called out.

"It's King. Open up."

I froze and stopped dead in my tracks.

"King, please leave," I said nervously.

"Jazzy, open the door. I need to talk to you." His voice sounded shaky.

I tiptoed up to the door and peered through the peephole. I was at a loss for words when I saw that he was crying. In all the years that I'd been with King, I'd never seen him cry.

"Talk to me about what?" I said with my back pressed against the door.

"Baby, I'm sorry, so sorry. I'm in trouble, baby. Please open the door," he whimpered.

Taking a deep breath, I turned the lock, then pulled the door open. King was still in his suit from yesterday. He looked a mess. I could sense that something was definitely wrong. He took a step forward and fell into my arms, sobbing like a baby.

"King, what's the matter?" I was starting to panic. I had never seen him like this.

"Jasmine, I fucked up and I'm sorry. Please forgive me, baby. Please forgive me," he begged. I guided him over to the sofa.

"It'll be okay, whatever it is," I said, now wiping my own tears. I didn't know why I was crying, but the shit was contagious.

"No, baby, you've got to say you forgive me." He looked up at me.

Choosing my words carefully, I said, "King, I forgive you, but I can't forget that easily. You put your hands on me and publicly humiliated me. To top it off, you let Danielle shit on me in the media."

"Baby, I swear I will never put my hands on you again, and I didn't let Danielle do anything. You know Danielle. I wasn't answering my phone, and neither were you, so she took control of the situation." He sniffled and finally stopped crying. "Jazzy, I know you're the only one who has my back besides God and Moms, so it's time for me to come clean. I need to tell you something." He looked into my eyes.

I stood from the couch on defense mode. "King, it better not be another woman or no babies."

"Jazzy, it ain't shit like that. I came here to confess that, for the past two years, I've been sniffing cocaine," he confided in me.

"You've been what?" I said.

"That's why I've been acting strange. I need help and didn't realize it until yesterday when I did what I did. I had just done a line with Melissa Valentine and was blowed out of my mind. I didn't realize what I'd done until last night when I was coming down from my high." He began to sniff again. "Jazzy, I've been trying to hide my habit, but it's taking over and starting to control me."

"How did you let this happen?" I asked in disbelief. King never even smoked weed, and now he was sniffing coke.

"It all started when I was doing my junior album, *Money Over Everything*. I was up late, sleeping about two hours a day for two months straight. Right after that, we left for promotional road shows. State after state, it was the same story—radio interviews in the morning, magazine spreads late afternoon, sound checks before performances, and of course, fans think you on some other shit if you ain't at the after-party. It just became too much. One day, some industry cat came through and told me all of my problems would be solved. He gave me a sample, and from there I was hooked. Once a month turned into every two weeks, which ended up being every day. Now I can't function without it."

I saw the pain in his eyes and felt his sadness in my heart. I couldn't imagine what King had been going through, but it did shed light on a lot of things.

"Jazzy, I need help." He put his head down in my lap. "Can you help me?" he asked.

"You know I'm going to help, baby. Now let's get you cleaned up." I helped him remove his suit and step into the bathwater that was still waiting for me. I washed my man and told him everything would be okay. I also recommended checking into rehab, but he refused.

"If I have to go cold turkey, I want to do it at home with you by my side," he said.

I was leery, but as we lay in bed that night, he reassured me he was going to kick this habit, and I believed him.


The flight home was wonderful. I was too excited to be back on Michigan soil. As promised, my girl Stacey was front and center, waiting curbside to pick me up. I

ignored the scowl on her face when she saw King beside
me, as I was sure she ignored my frown at the sight of her
sister riding shotgun. She popped her trunk so we could
put our bags inside. After tipping the gentleman who
helped bring our luggage to the car, we got into the back
of the car. Without a word exchanged between anyone,
not even Stace and me, she pulled off and headed in the
direction of our home.

"How was your trip? Did anything interesting happen?"
Tracey snickered.

I caught a glimpse of Stacey in the rearview and rolled
my eyes. *Why did she bring this hood bugger anyway?*
I reached over and squeezed King's hand. He smiled and
continued to peer out of the window.

Within thirty minutes, we were at my gate, and I was
punching the code. "Thank God," I mumbled under
my breath. Stacey drove up the circular driveway and
stopped right in front of the steps between two stone
lion-head statues.

"Thanks, girl, for the ride." I reached in the car window
and tried to hug her, but she was stiff.

"Jasmine, I thought you were done with this," she
whispered as King retrieved our luggage.

"It's a long story. I promise I'll call you in a few days," I
explained.

"A few days?"

"I'll explain everything in a day or two. Please just
understand," I begged. With that, she put her car in gear,
pulled off, and left me standing there.

"Jazzy, I told you I don't like that ho," King hollered. I
simply shook my head because the feelings between the
two of them were definitely mutual.

I stepped inside the foyer and was greeted by the
aroma of something from down South. My mother was
from Alabama and could throw down on some soul food.

"Mama, what are you cooking?" I just knew she was the one in the kitchen.

"I made some fried catfish, smothered pork chops, string beans, collard greens, baked sweet potatoes, macaroni and cheese, potato salad, corn muffins, and hot water bread." Removing her apron, she waved her hand like a model across the spread of food sitting along the granite countertops.

"Why did you make so much food?" I asked while kissing Jordan. He was at the table in his special wheelchair/high chair.

"Well, baby girl," she said, smiling, "me and Jordan think you guys need some alone time. I know you can't boil water, so I wanted to make enough for a few days. Jordan is going to stay with me so Mommy and Daddy can relax. Isn't that right, J-man?" She tickled Jordan, causing him to laugh.

Before our flight this morning, I called and told her everything about the cocaine and how King wanted to kick the habit without rehab. She probably figured things could potentially get ugly and Jordan didn't need to be present.

"Thanks, Wanda." King hugged my mother. "See you later, Jordan." He waved at our son, and I swallowed hard. He had never hugged or kissed Jordan. It was almost like he was scared to touch him.

I thanked my mom again for everything and walked them to the car. After kissing Jordan one last time, I waved them off. Turning to face the house, I released an audible breath. The next few days were going to be challenging. I rolled up the sleeves on my Yves Saint Laurent blazer, prepared for war. I was going to bring the man I fell in love with back to life because I was tired of this impersonator.

# Chapter Nineteen

## *Tionne*

The meeting at the lawyer's office had me so far down in the dumps that Zuri had to call in reinforcements to try to cheer me up. "Divas," my friend Lyric sang as she approached our table. We were sitting at the back booth of Charlie's Place, a gourmet diner not far from my hotel.

"Hey, girl." Zuri stood for a hug, but I remained seated. The three margaritas that I'd guzzled thirty minutes earlier were playing tricks with my vision and balance.

"Damn, T, you started the party without me?" She took a seat beside me, then wrapped her arm around my shoulder. "Girl, it's going to be all right."

"I gave him everything I had to build his empire, but I get nothing in the end." I knew the other day my mission was to leave with what I'd come with. However, after a few nights of thinking, I remembered that Dallas had also come with nothing. We built everything we had together. Why didn't I deserve a parting gift? "Y'all, I didn't even want half. I just wanted something to get me by until I could start my own company and make my own money."

"Do you have any private accounts, secret stashes, or anything that you could sell?" Lyric asked.

"No." I shook my head before grabbing the remainder of Zuri's cocktail and taking it to the head. "I can't believe

I was such a naive little bitch who thought my marriage would outlast this industry."

"Tionne, don't beat yourself up." Lyric patted my hand. "We've all played the naive position a time or two."

"Why is being the wife of a celebrity so goddamn hard?" Life was much better when things were simple. "You give a nigga a little fame and fortune, and they go crazy."

"I'll toast to that." Zuri raised one of the freshly filled beverages from the trio the waiter had just placed on the table. Lyric and I followed suit.

"Amen." I swigged my drink, then wiped my mouth with the back of my hand.

"Did y'all hear about Jasmine James and KJ?" Lyric asked. "T, that's your girl, right?"

"Yeah, she's my people. We actually went to high school together." I nodded. The news feed on my phone had been blowing up all day about the craziness that went down last night. "I tried to give her a call earlier, but she won't answer." I just wanted to show her some love since she was so far away from home, but I knew firsthand how it was when you didn't feel like being bothered.

"She probably booked the first flight back to Detroit." Zuri looked up from her phone. I guessed she was checking out the story. "I know I would have."

"Maybe I should go home and check on her."

"What? Why would you want to go there?" Zuri frowned.

"Girl, I saw some pictures online. That place looks scary as hell." Lyric shook her head.

"First of all, y'all bitches better back up off the D. There are still some nice areas. The media chooses to only show the blighted areas of my city." I loved my birthplace so much that I had a small tat under my left breast that read, "Est. In Detroit."

"Well, you can have the D or whatever you call it. I'll stay my ass right here in sunny California." Lyric laughed.

"Fuck you." I giggled.

"See?" Lyric pointed at me. "Detroit breeds them gangsters."

We all burst into laughter.

"Seriously though, I think I'll just call her again," I said, suddenly remembering that I no longer had the luxury of booking flights whenever I felt like it. "Besides, she may not feel up to any company right now."

"Poor thing probably needs a vacation," Lyric added.

"I know I need one," I agreed.

"Me too." Lyric raised her glass.

"Well, this is perfect timing." Zuri smiled. "I wanted to invite you girls on a trip to Puerto Rico," she sang. "Tionne, if you speak to Jasmine, please extend the invite to her as well. Although I don't really know her, I do know that the RWA has to stick together."

"What's the RWA?" I frowned, trying to figure out the acronym.

"Rich Wives Association." Zuri laughed.

"I like that one." Lyric giggled.

"Tramp, don't take my shit and tell people you made it up." Zuri pointed across the table. The alcohol was finally starting to affect them, but my ass had been wasted.

"Tell me more about this trip. How many days?" I was excited.

"Girl, I'm talking about five nights on the beach just maxing and relaxing."

Immediately, I noticed Lyric tense up. "How much will it cost?" she asked hesitantly.

"This is an all-expenses-paid trip, boo."

"Are you serious?" I'd known Zuri to buy a bitch a nice bag or a pair of shoes a time or two, but never had she treated Lyric and me to a vacation. "Thank you, Z!" I jumped up and hugged my girl.

"Don't thank me. Thank Jason." Zuri fingered the rim of her glass.

"Must be nice to have a husband like that," Lyric mumbled. She didn't really talk to us about her situation with Damien, but we'd heard through the grapevine that her money was a little funny lately.

"Don't do that, Lyric." Zuri wagged her finger.

"I'm just saying it must be nice to have a fine-ass husband who spoils you and remains faithful. I mean, I got two out of three, but you got a blessing." Lyric laughed.

"I said the same thing." I slapped her five, much to Zuri's dismay.

"Y'all bitches don't know half my struggle." Zuri continued playing with the rim of her glass.

"All we know is what we see, and damn it, your life looks good from this side of the table." Lyric raised her hand to her eyebrows, then turned her head from side to side as if she were looking for something. We all cracked up at her theatrics, even Zuri, but that didn't stop her from throwing us the middle finger.

"You two bitches are hilarious. Y'all need your own reality show." I wiped the tears from my eyes. They had me crying.

"Fuck that. I will never, ever do a reality show as long as I live." Zuri rolled her eyes. "They make everyone look like clowns or gangsters, and I'm not either. I have way too much class to sell myself for a fucking check."

"Yeah, I can't do it either." I shook my head. "There is no way I could imagine watching my life play out on television. Could y'all imagine a camera crew sitting here with us while I'm a drunken mess?" Grabbing Lyric's glass, I tipped it up. "I can see it now. Under my name it would read, 'the Alcoholic.' Nah, I'm good."

"Funny you should mention that." Lyric went into her clutch and laid a check on the table.

"Who the fuck is Linda Schmidt?" I slurred.

"She's the face behind all the reality television shows we've been bombarded with these past few years," Lyric informed us.

"No, you didn't!" Zuri's mouth was wide open.

"I didn't, I swear." Lyric raised her hands.

"So how did you get the check?" I asked with my lips twisted.

"I was styling a client who will be on her new show, and Linda was there. She gave me a check. I'm supposed to be thinking about it."

"I know she didn't insult you with this chump change," Zuri snapped. "Besides, I heard Linda Schmidt is bad news. Several of her cast members have filed lawsuits against her company for twisting their words and causing beef that leads to attacks on air by other cast members."

I didn't think more than a quarter million dollars was chump change, especially now that I was flat broke, but I did agree with Zuri about not doing the show. "I don't think you should do it, Lyric. You've kept your private life private all this time. Don't switch up now."

"You're right." Lyric stared at the lump sum check shortly before ripping it to pieces and tossing the confetti into her empty glass. "No amount of money is worth jeopardizing my family, my company, or my character," she declared.

I knew it was a huge decision for her to make, especially in times of need. Nevertheless, ultimately, she thought with her head and not her purse.

"So anyway, back to my trip! Are y'all bitches down or what?"

"Hell yeah," Lyric and I sang in unison.

"Let's leave on Monday. The sooner the better."

"Puerto Rico here we come." I beckoned the waiter for another round of drinks.

# Chapter Twenty

## *Diamond*

"Babe, where did you say you were going again?" Ken asked from the shower. He'd been home all day, and I was a little irritated. Normally, I loved having my man around, but today I had to shoot some moves. His ass was holding me up.

"I called Lyric. We're going shopping for a few hours." It was a bald-faced lie, but it bought me some time to do what I needed to do.

"Don't spend all my money." Ken laughed.

"Don't worry, I will," I yelled through the closed door.

"I got a few dollars in my sock drawer. Take all of it."

"Thanks, boo." I walked over to the drawer and began rummaging. Right away, I spotted a white envelope with several hundred dollars inside. The outside of the envelope had the amount $17,000 written on it. I was about to close the drawer when I noticed a checkbook. As soon as I grabbed it, Ken's voice boomed from the bathroom.

"I can't wait to show you off to my family. I know my country-ass cousins have never seen a chick like you."

"Shit." I clutched my heart. He'd scared me to death. "I can't either, boo." Without delay, I snatched a blank check from the back of his checkbook and tucked it into the back pocket of my jeans. I hated to steal from Ken, but desperate times called for desperate measures. Besides, I knew Ken was a multimillionaire. He would hardly miss anything I withdrew from his account.

"Be back in a few," I yelled before closing the drawer and making a mad dash to the door. Once inside of my car, I called my brother.

"Hello."

"Dexter, I'm on my way over to your friend's crib now. Are you sure he's legit?"

"Yeah, Omar is a cool dude. I told him you had the goods. He said he would give you twelve thousand." He spoke close into the receiver of his phone.

When I called Dexter the other day to see how I could get rid of the heroin, he told me about Omar, a big-time dope boy he did business with every now and then. "Twelve? I need at least twenty."

"Girl, ain't nobody gon' pay you top dollar for a hookup because then it wouldn't be a hookup." Dex laughed. "Besides, niggas like Omar don't even fuck with people he don't know. He's only doing business with you because you're my sister."

"I guess it'll have to do. I'm on my way over there now."

"Diamond, please be careful. This shit isn't pretend. These are real niggas you're about to encounter," Dexter warned. My brother had been in the dope game all my life. By now, he should've known I was used to drugs, guns, police, and killers.

"I'm a big girl. I can handle my own." Without another word, I ended the call, then headed over to see Omar.

During the ride, I could see Duck's Charger tailing me from two cars behind. Completely annoyed, I pulled up into a gas station and waited for him to do the same. As soon as he pulled into the parking space beside me, I rolled down my window and let him have it. "I told you to quit fucking following me. You're blowing my cover."

"And I told you that I keep close watch on my money."
Duck grimaced.

"When I get it, I'll be in touch. Until then, back the fuck
off." I rolled up the window, released my foot from the
brake, and peeled out of there on two wheels. Duck tried
to catch up, but it was useless. By the time he was back
on the street, he couldn't see shit but the dust my car had
left behind.

Nearly twenty minutes after losing him, I pulled up to
a nice home on a decent street. There was a flower bed,
the grass was mowed, and the hedges were trimmed.
A nice Cadillac rested in the driveway as well as a few
toys. Thinking I had the wrong address, I checked the
paper I'd written it down on against what I'd put in the
GPS. Surprisingly, this was the correct address. Hastily, I
grabbed my bag and approached the door. Before I could
knock, it swung open.

"Yes." The nose of a 9 mm handgun greeted me.

"Is Omar here?"

"Who wants to know?" The assassin brandishing the
weapon was a mixed woman with curly hair and a strong
bone structure.

"My name is Diamond." I stared her down, letting her
know I wasn't intimidated by her ice grill or pistol.

"Come on in." She stepped aside, allowing me to enter.
"My name is Isis. Omar left an hour ago, but he did say
you were coming by." She placed the gun behind her back
and tucked it into her jeans. "You got the shit?"

"Yeah, right here." I patted my bag. "You got the money?"

"It's all here." After she grabbed a large manila envelope from the coffee table, I reached into my purse and
handed her the vials still in the Ziploc bag. I watched
as Isis peered into the bag and nodded her approval. "It

looks good, but if it's not, Omar will want all of his money back."

"That shit is fire. Got the dopefiends going crazy in the city." One thing I knew how to do was bluff.

"It better be fire because Omar don't take kindly to con artists," Isis warned. "The last nigga who tried to pass off some wack shit came up missing, and he hasn't been found since."

I wanted to check her for using the word "nigga," but then I remembered she was the bitch holding the gun. "Try it if you don't believe me," I urged, fully praying and hoping the stolen dope was good.

"If need be, we'll be in touch." Isis nodded toward the door. That was my cue to put it in gear and get the hell out of there.

# Chapter Twenty-one

## *Jasmine*

After several long days and nights of vomiting, cold sweats, and nightmares, I wished like hell I'd taken Tionne's offer to join her and the other girls on the beach. I really appreciated her offer to come home and check on me, too, but my hands were full. Being on call all day and night was no easy feat. However, I could finally see the original King James begin to emerge. To say I was grateful would've been an understatement. His whole demeanor had changed in a week. He was more attentive to my needs and had even cooked dinner and catered to me last night. It felt like the old days with no distractions. No industry calls, no blogs to read, and no television to watch. We had taken a vacation from the world, and it felt great!

"Jazzy, I want tonight to be special, so pick out your best dress and flyest heels." He lay down on the pool chair next to me and grabbed my hand.

"What's the special occasion?" I smiled.

"Today is the day that I asked you to marry me all those years ago." He winked as I calculated the dates in my head.

"Baby, I can't believe you actually remember that." I was impressed.

"Jazzy, you're my rock, my world, and my foundation. Without you, I'm nothing, and I don't want to lose you."

"I'm not going anywhere, King." My voice was unsteady, and my hand was trembling.

"Now go take your fine ass upstairs and get ready. I got everything set up in the formal dining room. No peeking."

"Scout's honor," I said with my fingers crossed behind my back. I wasn't promising anything, and he knew I was going to peek. I had to see what he had prepared and what gifts were waiting for me.

"Oh, my God," I exclaimed. The sight was breathtaking. King had pulled out all the stops. I was beaming with excitement. This gesture proved that his love for me hadn't died. There were ten dozen roses in a variety of red, white, and pink scattered around the room. I took notice of all the boxes, which were strategically placed in every chair of the twelve-seat dining set.

"I thought I said no peeking," King said from behind me as he wrapped his strong arms around my waist.

"Baby, can I at least open one?" I was as bright-eyed as a kid on Christmas. King walked over to the head seat, then pulled the yellow-wrapped box from the chair.

"Only one though. After this one, go upstairs and get ready." He smiled as I pulled on the ribbon.

The sound of the doorbell stole our attention. "Who could that be? I'll be right back," I said, placing my gift down.

"I'll get it. You continue opening your gift." King placed the box back in my hand, then walked off. I tore into the pretty paper and gasped when I saw the diamond necklace, matching tennis bracelet, and ankle bracelet. They each had diamond-encrusted hearts hanging off of them. The necklace had King's name on the back, the tennis bracelet said, "Jordan," and the ankle bracelet was blank. Was King trying to give me a hint that he was ready to have a baby? The tears began to fall. I couldn't contain myself. Tonight would be the night I would tell him we were expecting.

"King, who was at the door?" I asked when he returned to the dining room.

"It was D-Bo," he said casually, but something in his voice concerned me. D-Bo was his bodyguard and right-hand man. He did anything for King. Sometimes, that wasn't a good thing.

"What did he want?" I raised an eyebrow.

"He brought over our flight details for tomorrow." He averted his eyes from me.

"Tomorrow?" I looked at him suspiciously. "Where are you going tomorrow?"

"The label wants to shoot this video for my next single in Atlanta. I should be gone no more than two days." He fumbled with his hands.

"Are you okay?" I finally spat it out because he was acting too awkward.

"Jazz, I'm good, girl. Now go upstairs and get ready." He playfully grabbed my ass. I did as I was told.

It took me two hours to get ready, but the end result was flawless. My makeup was gorgeous, and my hair was on point in a French roll and Chinese bangs. My skin was oiled and smelled of Juicy Couture. I had chosen a red Christian Dior spandex dress that fit like a glove all the way down to my ankles. The front of the dress dipped low in a V-cut that stopped just under my pierced navel. The back scooped off of my shoulders, exposing the cross that was tatted under my neck. My shoes were crystal-covered red bottoms. They went so well with the jewelry from earlier.

I made my way down the off-white spiraled staircase, then headed into the dining room. "Damn," King and I said in unison. He was standing there looking fresh to death in his custom black and burgundy Christian Dior three-piece suit. He pulled my chair out, then took the one to my left at the head of the table.

"You look beautiful, Mrs. James."

"Thanks, baby, and you look debonair," I said, filling my champagne flute with water.

"Tonight, I will be serving McDonald's." He lifted the brass lid that was covering my food. Sure as shit, there was an Angus burger and an order of fries. I cracked up laughing.

"What is this?"

"Well, I wanted to show you that I haven't forgotten where we come from." King smiled and leaned in for a kiss. "Jazzy, I'm all about new things and different experiences, but I never want to forget what made me who I am. You loved me when this was all I could afford, and that means so much to me. I love having you in my life, and I look forward to growing old with you." He raised his flute. "Here's to our future."

"Speaking of our future"—I nervously raised my flute—"we're having another baby." I clinked glasses with him and held my breath.

"Say what?" He scooted back from the table.

"I'm pregnant, King." I smiled, but the look he gave me was deadly.

"See, bitch, you just like the rest of them hoes out to get my money. A nigga blows up, then y'all start poking holes in condoms and shit. What the fuck am I going to do with another baby, Jasmine?"

"King, I just thought it would be nice for Jordan to have someone to play with." I tried to keep an even tone, but I was slowly registering what he had just said.

"Jordan is four and don't even know his own name, so how in the fuck is he going to play with some-damn-body?" His fists hit the marble table, causing me to flinch.

"Don't you talk about my son like that!" Now I was up and out of my seat. It was one thing to disrespect me but a whole different thing to disrespect my baby.

"What, Jasmine? You know what I'm saying is true. Your son is a fucking retard, and it's all your fault." King shook his head in disgust.

"How can you say that? Especially when he's your son too? Jordan is a person with feelings, not a retard. You treat him like shit, and he feels it. It hurts. How in the hell could you talk about your only son that way?" I was boiling hot and had reached for the butter knife on the table before I realized it.

"Oh, shit." He laughed. "You gon' stab me?"

"You better not let one more bad word about my son come from your mouth, or I just might stab you." My hand was trembling.

"As of tomorrow, your pregnant ass and your son need to find another place to stay. I got five kids already, and I for damn sure don't need any more." He said it like he hadn't just dropped a bomb on me.

"Five kids? Who in the hell are the other four?" I felt weak and tried to hold myself up by holding on to the back of the chair.

"Don't act brand new. You knew I was fucking around. I got Prince, Princess, King Jr., and Queenisha." He smiled, obviously proud of his offspring. "Shit, I got the whole royal family. All my kids are going to be something, too."

I watched as he pulled a folded piece of aluminum foil from his back pocket. He opened it up and sniffed. No wonder he was wilding out. His ass was getting high again.

*I bet D-Bo brought that shit to him earlier.*

"How can you be so fuckin' evil? You're the devil. I should've left your ass a long time ago." Although the tears were falling, I was numb to the pain.

"But you didn't, did you?" King removed his suit jacket. "Part of the reason that I stay with your dumb ass is because you take everything that I dish out." He laughed and I winced. "I fuck hoes, then come home to you with the juices on my dick from the next bitch, and you still suck it because you ain't got no other choice."

"Fuck you, King." I gripped the butter knife like it was a machete. "You better not come any closer." I was about to murder this nigga. Not only had he just confirmed his many affairs with multiple women, but he had also admitted to having children, two of which belonged to that bitch Tracey. "You ain't nothing but a piece of shit. I'm sorry that I ever loved you." I wiped my eyes.

"Yeah, yeah. That's what they all say," I heard him mumble as I ran upstairs.

# Chapter Twenty-two

## *Lyric*

Before I knew it, the Puerto Rico trip was here, and I was ready to go. The kids were off to school, and Damien had gone to the gym. Knowing his new movie was about to begin filming, Damien had been working out like a maniac. I was so happy to see him doing something productive with his time and mind. Finally, things were beginning to look better for my family, and I was thrilled. Just as I closed the zipper on my carry-on, my cell phone rang.

"Hello."

"Hey, Lyric, it's Diamond. Are you busy?"

"Kind of, but what's up?" I always wanted to make my clients feel like a priority even when I had a million things going on.

"Good. Girl, I need you to meet me on Rodeo Drive now. Ken is taking me to meet his family this week, and I don't have anything mother-approved in my closet." Diamond sounded worried.

"Right now?" Looking down at the watch on my wrist, I saw I only had three hours before I was set to leave for the airport with Tionne.

"It shouldn't take long. All I need are a few pieces for Alabama."

"Okay," I sighed, knowing damn well I was pushing it. However, I didn't want to decline Diamond's request when her boyfriend had me on retainer. "I'm leaving the house now. I'll meet you at Gucci."

After loading my bags into the trunk of my car, I headed out to meet her on Rodeo Drive. As soon as I started the engine, my phone started ringing again. This time, it was my mother. "Hey, Mama."

"Don't 'hey' me. Why haven't you paid my car note?"

"Excuse me?" I didn't like the way she was talking to me.

"I said, 'Why haven't you paid my car note?' The repo man had the audacity to try to take my shit at the country club in front of everyone." My mother only cursed when she was angry.

"Mama, I heard you the first time. I only said, 'Excuse me,' for how you came at me," I paused, trying my best to remain respectful toward my mother. "I didn't pay your car note because I could barely pay mine."

"Do you know I had to go in my purse and make a payment on the spot for them to take my car off the truck?" she continued as if I hadn't said a thing. "I had to give them five thousand dollars because of all the payments you missed."

"At least you had five thousand, goddammit!" I didn't mean to curse at my mother, but she had taken me to a new level of irritation.

"Have you lost your mind, Lyric Nicole?" She only used my middle name when I was in trouble. "Claud," she called for my father. "Your daughter done lost her mind. Pick up the phone."

"Hello," my father answered after fumbling with the second phone.

"Hey, Daddy."

"Hey, pumpkin." My daddy proceeded to ask about Damien and the kids but was cut off as usual by my mother.

"Forget all the greetings. Tell your father what you had the nerve to say to me."

"Mom, the only reason I said that is because you don't listen. I've been telling you for a while now that things are not looking good over here. I've tried to tell you that I'm robbing Peter to pay Paul, barely able to pay my bills, let alone yours too. I've tried telling you that I don't have any money, but all you hear is what you want to hear. Instead of asking me if I'm okay and what you can do to help, all I hear you say is, 'More, more, more.'"

Without another word, I pressed the end button and hung up on my parents. By now, the tears were falling down my face. For so long, I hadn't been heard, and it was beginning to wear me down. The entire family saw me as an ATM, ready and willing to dispense money at their request. I was tired of it all.

By the time I emerged from the car to meet Diamond, my tears had been replaced with a fresh coat of makeup. I was ready to do the job I'd been hired for.

"Thanks for coming on short notice." Diamond greeted me with a hug in front of the Gucci store.

"No problem." I embraced her back. "I only have three hours, but I'll get you right in less than two." Holding the door open, we waltzed in like we owned the joint.

"I'm so nervous, Lyric. I really want his mom to like me," Diamond admitted while eying a navy blazer.

"Just be yourself. If she likes you, fine. If she doesn't, it's her loss. After all, you don't want her falling in love with someone you're not, because then you'll have to keep up the facade forever."

"I never thought about it like that." Diamond nodded her head. "It's just that guys like Ken don't come around often, and I don't want to lose him on account of his mother."

"I know what you mean, but you can't worry about it. Ken loves you, and that's all that matters." Immediately, I was drawn to a cream-colored casual lounge ensemble with "Gucci" written on it in gold cursive letters. "I think you would look stunning in this on the airplane." I held it up to her.

"Um . . ." The way her lips were twisted, I could tell this wasn't her taste. "What about this?" She flew over to a pair of leopard skinny jeans and a matching top. "Gucci" was written on it in red. It wasn't my thing, but I wasn't the client.

"It could work, provided you have the right shoes."

"I like these." Diamond grabbed the matching leopard boots off a display nearby.

"I think that's too much leopard." I shook my head. "How about you buy the top and the shoes, then pair them with black jeans instead?"

"I like that." She put the leopard pants back, and we continued shopping.

Next, we stopped in Bebe, then Juicy. After grabbing several pieces, we ended the day at Neiman Marcus. For almost the entire time we shopped, I noticed a guy lurking not too far behind us.

"Girl, I'm about to alert security."

"What's wrong?" Diamond looked up from the chair she was sitting in.

"Have you noticed this guy following us from store to store?" I pointed at the creep pretending to look at the YSL purses on display.

"Shit." She stood abruptly, knocking over her bag in the process. "Give me a second." Diamond waltzed over to the guy and started going ham. I couldn't hear what she was saying, but it was obvious the two of them knew each other. I tried not to stare, so I busied myself picking up the contents of her purse.

"What the fuck?" I frowned. On the floor were several blouses from the Gucci store with tags on them.

"Sorry, Lyric. That was my old boyfriend," Diamond said before noticing her shit on the floor. "Why the fuck was you in my purse?" Quickly, she bent down and reloaded her bag with the hot goods.

"Girl, you knocked your bag over when you stood up. I was just picking your things up." I dropped one of the shirts and stood. "I'm out. I can't be associated with this." Grabbing my shit, I headed for the nearest exit.

"Lyric, wait up. Let me explain." Diamond was on my ass, but I wasn't stopping.

Just as we approached the front door, we were greeted by two police officers and an employee from the Gucci store. "That's them, Officer."

"Empty your bags."

"Excuse me?" Diamond snapped.

"Shit." I couldn't believe this was really happening.

"Open up the bags, or I will open them for you." One of the cops made a move for Diamond's purse, and she hit him with it. Next thing I knew, all four of us were getting physical.

"Stop it," I screamed. The male officers were forcefully pushing me and Diamond to the floor. "I didn't steal shit."

"We saw the tape!" the store clerk yelled as both officers slapped cuffs on me and Diamond. I watched as he went through my bag and then through Diamond's, where all of her stolen items came tumbling to the floor.

"Let's take a ride to the station." He lifted me to my feet.

"I didn't steal anything. I swear." I was practically crying now. Never had I been put in handcuffs and placed under arrest.

"Don't say shit, Lyric! I'm going to call Ken. He'll handle it," Diamond yelled as she was escorted to one of the waiting squad cars and I was escorted to the other.

# Chapter Twenty-three

## *Zuri*

"Baby, I just wanted to stop by and give you a kiss before the car service comes to pick me up for the airport," I said after opening the door to Jason's office down the hall from our bedroom. He was sitting in the oversized chair, talking on the phone.

"Are you fucking sure?" he barked, causing me to practically jump from my skin. Anytime he was on ten, I hated to be anywhere in the vicinity. "Fix this like I fucking pay you to do." Jason slammed the phone down and leaped from his seat so fast I didn't have time to exit.

"What happened?" I asked while being backed into a corner.

"Trent Cambridge signed with Phillip. I can't believe this shit!" With his teeth gritted, Jason sent a body shot right to my side. "After all I did for that boy, and he repays me by signing with my rival, making me lose out on a ten percent cut of thirty million dollars." Jason sent another blow to the same exact spot. This time, I dropped to the floor and balled up into the fetal position. "Get off the fucking floor. Your transportation will be here in a minute." Just like that, my husband stepped right over me, then waltzed out the door.

For nearly fifteen minutes, I lay in the same spot too weak to stand and too scared to call out for help. It wasn't until Sylvia came in from her afternoon walk and yelled for me that I finally spoke, "I'm in here."

"Girl, I just met that fine-ass neighbor of yours, Judge Pritchett. He may be y'all's new stepdaddy." She practically tripped over me in the doorway of the study. "Baby, what's the matter? Why are you on the floor?"

"Please just help me to the bathroom down the hall."

"Where is his black ass at?" she asked while carefully pulling me to my feet.

"I heard the front door close a few minutes before you came in. He probably went for a ride." I limped down the hall to the guest bathroom.

"Did he hurt you bad? Sit down on the toilet. Let me take a look."

"Ouch." I nearly jumped out of my skin as Sylvia tried to access the fresh bruises her son had applied to my rib cage.

"I think he may have broken something. You should see a doctor."

"I'll be fine." Taking a hold of the bathroom sink, I tried to pull myself up. It was hard to breathe, and my shit ached with tremendous pain.

"What happened this time?" Sylvia assisted me to my feet.

"One of the guys Jason was scouting for his sports representation agency signed a deal with his competition," I sighed.

"Enough is enough. Next time he'll kill you." Sylvia was livid. "I didn't raise him like this, Zuri." I could tell Syl was mortified by her son's actions.

"I know you didn't." I patted her hand before limping over to the master suite and scanning the vicinity for anything I forgot to pack. I'd had my moment to mope. Now it was back to business as usual.

"When he comes home, I'll have a long talk with that boy. You don't deserve this, baby." Syl seemed more shaken up than I was.

"Don't worry about me. A few days on the beach and I'll be just fine," I tried to reassure my mother-in-law.

"Zuri, I really wish you would see a doctor." Syl grabbed my hand just as the doorbell chimed.

"I'll be fine." With a smile, I grabbed my purse and cell phone and tried my best to make it down the stairs. Truth was, I wasn't fine. Not only was my body in pain, but my feelings were hurt. Although I pretended everything was okay, it wasn't. I was tired of being Jason's punching bag.

"Hey, girl," Tionne shouted from the foyer. The maid had let her in.

"Hey." I put on the biggest smile I could muster. "Are you ready for Puerto Rico?"

"Hell yeah." She started doing some dance that didn't have a name. "Where is Lyric?"

"I was just about to ask you the same thing. Wasn't she riding over with you?" With my hand gripping the stair rail for dear life, I made it down each one without revealing how much I was hurting.

"I've been calling her, and her phone keeps going to voicemail." Tionne pulled out her phone and called Lyric once more. "See? It went to voicemail again."

"I hope everything is okay."

"Me too." Tionne dialed again.

"I don't want to leave her, but I don't want to waste first-class tickets either." I laughed. "Let me text Leslie." Quickly, I shot a message to Lyric's daughter. Instantly, she texted back to let me know that her mom had a last-minute client. I relayed the information to Tionne, so we decided to meet Lyric at the airport. There was no sense in all three of us missing our flight.

On our way out the door, Jason's car pulled back up. My stomach did a somersault as he stepped out, but I remained cool.

"Hey, Jay." Tionne nodded and he nodded back. I purposefully walked past him to the rear of the car, where my daughter was sleeping peacefully. Not wanting to disturb her, I only blew a kiss in her direction, then backed away. I was definitely going to miss Jelly, but I needed space to think about my next move.

"Aren't you gon' say bye?" Jason wrapped his massive arm around my waist, causing me to flinch.

"Ouch," I whispered. "That hurts."

"I love you with every fiber of my being. You know that, right?" he whispered while releasing his embrace.

"I love you too," I replied. Both of our reflections were visible in the car mirror. I was sure he saw when I rolled my eyes.

"Come on, Z, let's roll." Tionne was turned all the way up.

"See you later." I pushed past my husband and made my way over to the waiting party bus ready to drop us off at the airport.

"Let's get the party started." Tionne was already inside pouring the chilled champagne as I climbed the three short stairs to the bus in agony.

"Amen," I replied, although I was no longer in party mode. I couldn't help but feel uneasy about everything. For the first time in forever, I was questioning my love for Jason and my loyalty to our marriage. Sometime between this time and the last time he put his hands on me, my outlook about it had changed. I no longer wanted to be on the receiving end of his blows. Things needed to change, and I was going to make sure of that the minute I returned home.

# Chapter Twenty-four

## *Diamond*

After we spent nearly five hours down at the police station, they finally agreed to let us go with a warning. All I had to do was pay for my shirts and never return to the Gucci store again. "What the fuck is wrong with you?" Lyric was pissed. "Why are you stealing when there is a fucking black card in your wallet?"

"I don't want to talk about it," I said as we collected her shoes and personal items from the front desk.

"Fine, don't talk to me, but Ken is going to want to know what your problem is right before he dumps your ghetto ass." She pointed to Ken on the other side of the door. He was casually resting on the bench in the waiting area beside Lyric's husband.

"Fuck." I hadn't even thought about what I would say when he got here. The only reason I even dialed his number was because I knew he was the only person I could rely on to bail me out. Thinking fast, I pushed past Lyric and made my way into the lobby.

"Babe, are you all right?" Ken stood. "What happened?"

"It was awful." I started crying. "Ken, I've never been to jail a day in my life. I feel so ashamed and embarrassed."

"What happened? Was it a misunderstanding?" Ken wrapped his long arms around me.

"I called Lyric to go shopping with me for Alabama, but I didn't know she was a thief."

"What?" Lyric, Damien, and Ken all said concurrently.

"Bitch, I may be a lot of things, but a thief isn't one of them," Lyric snapped. "Tell your man whose Birkin bag they pulled the Gucci tops from."

"Girl, stop. You know you put that shit in my purse." I put my hand in her face. "My man gave me plenty of money to go shopping with. You're the only broke bitch around here. So it looks like you're the only one with a motive to steal."

"Ken, I know you don't believe that." Lyric stepped to Ken.

"Lyric, I can't believe you would stoop to this level. We're done!"

"What?" She was flabbergasted. "Ken, are you serious? You know me."

"Listen, I can't be associated with this, and neither can my girl. I don't know what you and your husband are into, but we can't take part in that crazy shit." Ken looked down at Lyric.

"Fuck you, nigga. Don't nobody talk to my wife like that." Damien jumped up, but Lyric got in between them.

"Look, Lyric, I need my money back. If you can't afford to return it in full by Friday, then you might as well find an attorney, because I will be taking you to court." Ken grabbed my hand and pulled me toward the door. I wanted to laugh at how Lyric was about to cry. It was pathetic.

"Baby, please get me out of here." With my head down, I flew to Ken's car parked curbside.

Once inside, I continued to make up a colorful story about Lyric and her "thieving" ass. Ken felt bad that he had introduced me to such a character, and he apologized profusely. "I just hope they don't publish the story and your mother sees it along with my mugshot."

"Don't worry, baby. We'll explain everything if neces-
sary." Ken patted my knee.

With a smirk, I reclined in the seat and retrieved my
cell phone from my bag. During the time I'd been in the
holding cell, I'd missed ten calls. Most of the numbers
were unfamiliar, so I checked the messages.

"Bitch, when I see you, I'm going to kill you and your
boyfriend. You can run but you can't hide. I got eyes
everywhere." I didn't recognize the voice, but I knew it
had to be Omar. I had no idea why he was mad, but the
next message was from my brother. Hopefully, he would
give me some insight.

"Diamond, what the fuck, man? I vouched for you. Call
me back."

"What is going on?" I mumbled to myself. Ken was so
busy blasting his music that he wasn't paying me any
mind. It was a good thing, too, because as soon as the
third voicemail started playing and I heard Grace's voice,
my whole face hit the floor.

"Diamond, it's Grace. You know, it's hard to believe
me and you were once like sisters. I let you into my
home and you stole my shit?" Grace laughed. "Although
I could give less than a fuck about your skank ass, I
thought you should know all of those vials were filled
with small pieces of chipped soap, not heroin. You won't
get a dollar from that package, you bum bitch."

It was all starting to make sense now, and my stomach
was in a knot. My life was officially in danger, and I had
no one to blame but myself. Omar was surely going to
kill me for selling him $15,000 worth of chipped soap.
As much as I loved Ken, it was time to do what I did
best—hop on a plane and get ghost.

"Duck," Ken screamed.

"Huh?" Instantly, I looked up expecting to find the
piece-of-shit skeleton from my closet. Instead, what

I found was a blue Chevy riding extremely close. The driver of the vehicle held a large-caliber weapon out the window and started blasting.

The car was riddled with bullets. I could tell Ken was hit by the way he slumped over on me. Desperately, I tried to take hold of the steering wheel, but it was too late. We sped into an embankment and became airborne.

# Chapter Twenty-five

## *Tionne*

The entire ride to the airport was silent. Something was up with Zuri, and I knew it. "Hey, girl, are you all right?"

"Yeah, I'm good. Just thinking about life, you know." Zuri gulped down her drink and continued staring out of the window.

"What's wrong, Z? Talk to me." It was unlike her to be so detached. Every time we were together it was a party, but today seemed more like a funeral.

"Everything is wrong, Tionne, but you wouldn't understand."

"Me not understand?" I felt offended. "Don't you know what I've been going through lately? My husband is a cheater, and I don't have any money. I think I may be a little more understanding than you think," I said before smacking my lips.

"It's not like that, T."

"Well, what is it like then? We're best friends. You should be able to talk to me about anything. I tell you about everything." I was becoming frustrated.

"Tionne, no offense, but you tell me all of your business because you want to. Some things are private to me, and this is one of them." Zuri seemed to be getting irritated as well.

"Whatever, Zuri. I see how it is." With my arms crossed, I pulled out my phone and checked Instagram. "You know, sometimes I think you believe you're better than me." By now, the champagne was talking.

"Girl, bye." Zuri dismissed me with the wave of her hand.

"It's the truth," I retorted. "You have the perfect life with a perfect career, a perfect child, and perfect husband who gives you money and takes you on trips to places most people can't even pronounce. All of the stars aligned when you fell from between your mother's legs." I giggled. "Miss Fucking Perfect."

"Really, Tionne, we're going to go there?" Zuri stood from her seat on the moving party bus. "Well, tell me, Tionne, does living in a perfect world include getting my ass beat every goddamn time my perfect husband has a bad day?" With tears, Zuri lifted her shirt to not only show me the fresh bruises on her side, but the old wounds on her back.

"Z, I'm sorry." I was completely floored.

"Forgive me if I'm not so quick to tell you that my nose has been broken, my shoulder has been dislocated, or that my teeth have been knocked out. It's not exactly a goddamn conversation starter." Zuri wiped her face with the back of her hand.

"Please forgive me. I had no idea. Please forgive me." I went over and hugged my friend, who was crying hysterically. She sounded like a child as she gagged on her tears.

"I'm scared." Zuri sniffed. "One day, he will kill me, Tionne. What about Jelly?"

"No, he won't, I swear, because we're going to get you out of there." Now I was crying too. "We're going to turn this bus around and go home and get your shit."

"Jason won't let that happen." Zuri broke our embrace.

"We'll call the police if need be."

"No, I don't want him to get in any trouble." Zuri shook her head profusely.

"Fuck him," I spat. "I say we roll up in that bitch with five-o, grab Jelly and your things, and get ghost." The Detroit in me was emerging. As the saying goes, you can take the girl out of the hood, but you can't take the hood out of the girl.

"It's not that simple. If I do this the wrong way, Jason will make me pay severely for it."

"We can get you a restraining order, Z."

"Girl, bye, what is a piece of paper going to do to protect me?" Zuri looked at me sideways. "You know the type of pull being a celebrity has."

"You're right," I sighed, taking the seat beside her. Oftentimes, having star status put you above the law for a little hush money and an autograph.

"I need a plan, Tionne." Zuri rested her head in her lap.

"How about we cancel this girl's trip and go back to my hotel room to regroup?" Wrapping my arms around Zuri, I squeezed her tightly. I could only imagine what my friend had been enduring in the name of love. She was a good person who deserved much better. I felt guilty for thinking her life was a fairy tale when, in reality, she was trapped in a nightmare worse than mine.

"That's actually a good idea." Zuri popped her head up. "Jason has a big conference downtown tomorrow that should last about four hours. I can use that time to get my shit and get out before he comes back."

"Let's do the damn thing." I extended my hand for a pact.

"You don't have to go, Tionne. I don't want to drag you into my mess." Zuri shook her head.

"Bitch, me and you are down like four flats on a Cadillac!" There was no way I would send her into the lion's den alone. Jason couldn't whip both of us at the same time. Therefore, I was prepared for war.

# Chapter Twenty-six

## *Jasmine*

I lay awake in the guest suite down the hall from my bedroom all last night, replaying every single word exchanged between me and my husband. Not only had I come to the conclusion that King really probably never loved me, but I also reached the revelation that I was a joke to my best friend. Her nephew and niece were my motherfucking stepkids. That bitch Stacey had to know King was fucking around on me with her sister. For God's sake, Prince was four years older than Jordan, and Princess was six months younger.

My mind raced as I reminisced about the times we went on shopping trips or girls' weekends out of town. She was keeping my ass busy while her sister was probably over here playing house up in my shit. "That dirty trick," I said aloud as it finally hit me. The reason Tracey's ass was mini balling was because of King. My husband was the one footing her bills. He was either breaking her off or paying child support. That was how that heffa went and spent six stacks the other day. *"If I wanted King, I could've had him."* Her words echoed in my head. "Your gold-digging ass won't want him when I'm done," I said out loud to myself and laughed wickedly. I was about to make this bastard pay for all the years that I'd been living in hell.

After sliding on a black spaghetti-strap tank top and pulling on my black Juicy Couture bottoms with the gold lettering, I slipped on my gold metallic UGG boots and was out of the room in no time. I walked down the stairs and heard voices coming from the study.

"What time are we leaving for the airport?" I poked my head inside the door.

Both King and D-Bo stared as if they had seen a ghost. "Um, we?" King looked confused.

"Yeah, we. I want to ride with you to the airport since I won't be seeing you for a few days." I smiled and he frowned.

"Yo, D-Bo, let me holler at Jasmine right quick, big dog." He leaned back in the oversized leather swivel chair.

"No problem, boss. I'll be outside." D-Bo walked his 311 pounds lightly past me like his ass was walking on eggshells. "Morning, Jasmine."

"D-Bo," was all I gave him along with a slight nod. I walked into the warm neutral-colored space, then pulled the French doors closed.

"Are you okay?" King scratched his forehead.

"Couldn't be better." I smiled, flashing all of my pearly whites. "How are you this morning?"

"I'm good." He cleared his throat. "Look, Jazzy, about last night, I—"

"What about last night?" I waved my hand. "It's old news, right? I mean, you did say everything you needed to say, didn't you?"

"Um, yeah, I guess, but—"

"But nothing. It's water under the bridge. Now what time is that flight?"

"I actually need to be leaving now." King stood from the chair in his navy blue Sean John sweatsuit.

"Well, let's hit the road. We don't want you to miss it." Quickly, I spun around and proceeded to the front door.

The minute this asshole was in the sky, I was coming back here and cleaning him out.

Minutes later, we were on our way. "Damn, D-Bo, slow down before we get pulled over," King called from the back seat. I had to admit, D-Bo was pushing it, but the quicker we got King to the airport, the happier I would be.

"Boss, you only got twenty minutes before the plane leaves. We need to get there," he insisted.

"Arrive alive! Ain't you ever heard that saying?" King reached up and held on to the handle we used for hanging our dry cleaning up.

"We're almost there, boss." We bent a few more corners, flew over a pothole or two, and blew a red light right in front of a cop.

"Damn." I was the one who spoke up this time. Just as I feared, lights began to flash, and the sirens blared.

"Nigga, if I miss this flight, that's your job," King threatened. D-Bo pulled over just as the officer had instructed over the speaker. Slowly coming to a stop with the police officer on our bumper, we sat there in silence.

"Jazz, let me see your purse," King spoke as the officer stepped from the sheriff's vehicle.

"Why?" I asked.

"I need to put my phone in there."

"Why?" I asked again.

"Because," he said, clenching his teeth, "these officers will fuck with me after they recognize who I am. The last time I was pulled over, they searched the car and took my phone."

"What's so special about your phone?" I was still confused.

"It ain't about the phone. It's about what's in it. You know how many other celebrities' numbers and addresses I got in my phone. I got a lock on it, but nowadays people can hack into everything."

Not thinking twice about it, I handed over my Dooney & Bourke seconds before the officer tapped on the door.

"License, insurance, and registration, sir," he said while looking back at us. D-Bo handed over the items. Then the older African American officer reviewed them thoroughly. "Son, do you know why I pulled you over?"

"'Cause I'm black?" D-Bo responded with much attitude. Was his big ass blind? The officer was as black as midnight his damn self.

"Don't get cute with me, son."

"I ain't your son," D-Bo added. I was about to pass out in the back seat. *No, he didn't just say what I think he said.*

"What's with the attitude, and why did you run that red light?" the officer asked.

"I'm trying to get my boss to the airport, and I don't have an attitude."

"You realize you could've killed someone back there?" The officer removed his sunglasses.

"Wasn't nobody coming when I blew that light, and you know it." D-Bo was working my nerves and, by the looks of it, King's too.

"Officer, I apologize for my driver's behavior. Today is his first day, and I think he's a little nervous." King rolled his window down and lied with a straight face.

"Hey, aren't you that fella from the television?" The officer peered at King.

"Yes, sir! My name is King James, but you may know me as KJ." King extended his hand, which the officer shook.

"Yeah, KJ. My grandkids watch your videos all the time. I've seen one or two myself, and I want you to know that they sicken me." He frowned.

"Excuse me?" King said.

"All you talk about is sex and drugs. It's very distasteful, son. You disrespect our women and teach our children that it's okay to sell and use drugs." He shook his head.

"Old man, are you done talking? We got places to be," D-Bo chimed in, causing me to roll my eyes. He had struck a nerve with the officer.

"Everybody, step from the vehicle now." Right after he said that, he drew his weapon. We jumped from the car with our hands up. "Have a seat over there on the sidewalk. If one of you moves, you're all going to jail."

My heart damn near jumped from my chest as he searched D-Bo's Trailblazer. I didn't know what he was liable to find on the inside of that thing, but I was silently praying that it was nothing that would land us in jail. No one made a sound as the officer headed back over to us. I didn't know if it was me, but he seemed to be going in slow motion as he carried my purse.

"Ma'am, could you step over here for a second?"

On wobbly legs, I took five long steps toward him. "Yes, sir?"

"This is your bag, correct?" He held it up and I nodded.

"Yes, sir, that's my purse." I felt a lump form in my throat.

"Please turn around for me, and place your hands behind your back. You're under arrest," he said with force, although his face read disappointment.

"Why am I being arrested?" I asked over my shoulder. He secured the cuffs, then turned me around to face him.

"You're being arrested for the possession of narcotics. Does this look familiar?" He waved a sandwich bag in front of my face. It looked like baby powder and reminded me of what King was sniffing last night.

"That's not mine, Officer," I screamed.

"Possession is nine-tenths of the law, baby," King called from the sidewalk with his cell phone glued to his ear. It was the same cell phone that he had asked to put in my purse. That was when I realized I had been set up by my own fucking husband.

After the officer read me my rights, I was placed in the back of the squad car. I looked on as he handed D-Bo a ticket along with his other documentation.

"Jasmine, I'll be back in two days, okay? Just hang tight, baby." With that said, I watched as my husband threw me the deuces and pulled off to go shoot his music video in Atlanta. I shook my head in disbelief. This nigga had just left me stuck with a damn possession charge.

"Ma'am, can I call anyone for you?" the officer asked. "Sometimes you're not given a phone call until they finish booking you and processing your information. It could be hours, and you look like a nice girl. I would hate for you to have to wait that long," the officer explained.

"Thank you, sir. Can you call my mother?" I rattled off the number to her home phone. When she didn't pick up, I gave the officer her cell number, but she didn't answer that either.

"Maybe your boyfriend will get a hold of her." He made eye contact with me through the rearview mirror.

"That's my husband, and I doubt it," I mumbled.

"That guy is your husband?" He became wide-eyed. "And he just left you like this?" he said while shaking his head. "You young people never cease to amaze me." He chuckled while I frowned.

"Look, I was leaving him today. As soon as he got on the plane, I was packing up me and my son, and we were out." I didn't know why, but I felt as if I had to explain myself.

"Is that right?"

I could tell by his tone that he didn't believe me for one second, but I was dead serious.

As we pulled into the police station, which was about two miles from the airport, my stomach began to ache. I wasn't sure if it was the baby, hunger pains, or the fact that I was nervous as hell. Aside from watching the show *Cops* on TV, I had never been up close and personal with the law. The officer came around to open my door and help me out of the car. I looked at his name tag, which read "Sheriff Johnson."

"Okay, this is it. We're here."

The place resembled a small office and was a little too spiffy to be for the bad guys. The waiting area looked cozy and smelled of fresh paint. The linoleum floors were waxed and shining. There was also a fresh smell in the air. I was pleased that since I had to be taken to jail, at least it was this one.

"What's going on, Frank?" the female officer behind the receptionist desk asked after looking up from her *Sloppy Gossip* magazine.

"Nothing much, Lizzie. This is Mrs. Jasmine James. She's being charged with possession of cocaine." Frank leaned on the counter as I cringed at what he had just said. Officer Lizzie glanced up at me then back down at her magazine.

"Are you King James's wife?" She looked bewildered. I started to say no, but maybe saying yes would work in my favor. Sheriff Johnson was old school and by the book. Perhaps this 30-something lady would let me pass for an autograph, picture, free CD, or something.

"Yes. That's me." I stood tall, flung my hair over my shoulder, and tried to appear as glamorous as she probably thought I was.

"Wow. This is not your week, huh?" She turned her magazine toward me. You could have bought me for a penny. I was too done. Right there, smack dab in the middle of the page, was a picture of me on the floor being pulled by King. My mouth was wide open, my makeup was a mess, and there was a huge red star covering my exposed private part. The title of the article was YOUNG & RECKLESS.

"Not my week at all." I was too ashamed to look her in the face, so I looked down at the floor instead.

Right after the humiliating moment, I was handed over to Officer Lizzie and taken to the back for booking. "Hold this sign and look straight ahead. Turn left. Now turn right," she instructed.

I knew my mug shots would hit the internet by tomorrow, so I tried my best to look fabulous. After the photo shoot, I was fingerprinted, drug tested, and allowed my phone call. "Praise the Lord and leave a message." My mother's voicemail came on, and I rolled my eyes. Where was she when I needed her?

"Hey, Mama, it's me. I got into some trouble, and I need you to bail me out." I rattled off the address and phone number of the precinct before hanging up the beige desk phone.

"Would you like to call King?" Lizzie asked like she knew him and we were cool like that.

"He's out of town," I sighed.

"What about a lawyer? Rich people keep those on standby," she commented.

"The only lawyer we have is an entertainment lawyer, and she's out of Georgia," I explained. Truth be told, even if the bitch were around the corner, I didn't have a number to reach her at. She was King's attorney, and I had only met her once at a fundraiser.

"What about friends?"

I looked at her and almost broke into tears as I thought about Stacey. Other than my mother, she was the only person in my life I knew for sure had my back. Up until last night, I thought she was my one true-blue friend. Boy, was I wrong.

"Nope, no friends either," I replied.

"Okay, well, maybe your mom will get the message and call you back." Lizzie almost looked sorry for me.

We walked down a short hallway and stopped in front of a door marked HOLDING. "Can't I just post my own bail?" I asked, remembering hearing something like that on one of my TV shows. I needed to get the hell out of here and fast. I only had two days to work with before King was back. By the looks of it, I'd be here for at least a few more hours.

"You won't be given a bond until tomorrow morning. You'll go before the judge, and he'll set it then." Lizzie unlocked the white door.

"Tomorrow?" I repeated, and she nodded. Losing a day would really put a damper on my plans, but I was determined to leave King and teach those no-good twins a lesson before Jordan, my mom, and I left town. I needed a fresh start and a new beginning.

# Chapter Twenty-seven

## *Diamond*

All night I had tossed and turned on the chair in the hospital lobby, and I awoke with a stiff neck. Ken had been rushed to surgery with several gunshot wounds to various parts of his body. Miraculously, I only sustained minor cuts and bruising. One of the bullets had pierced my arm, but other than a few stitches, I was fine.

"Miss, were you the one in the car with Mr. Tucker?" one of the two men who approached me asked.

Right off the bat, I knew they were detectives. Surprisingly, they hadn't shown up to question me yesterday when it all happened. However, I knew it was coming sooner or later.

"Yes, my name is Diamond. Ken is my fiancé. Is he okay?" The hospital hadn't divulged any information to me yet because I wasn't immediate family.

"Unfortunately, we're unable to give up details at this time." The officer patted my shoulder before taking a seat beside me. His partner continued standing with notepad and pen in hand.

"I am his fucking fiancée. I deserve to know if he's dead or alive."

"Calm down, Ms. Diamond. I didn't mean to upset you. Off the record, Mr. Tucker is alive." The officer extended his card. "My name is Officer Kemp, and this is Officer

Brown. We were assigned to your fiancé's case. Can you recount yesterday for me?"

"I already told the cops on the scene I didn't see shit." I rolled my eyes.

"Ms. Diamond, I didn't ask you what you saw. I simply asked you to recount the day's events." Officer Kemp calmly chewed on a piece of gum while staring me down. This wasn't his first rodeo, but it wasn't mine either.

"Ken had just picked me up, and we were heading home. I was looking at my phone when the car went airborne. I thought we had been in a car accident until the paramedics said otherwise."

"What happened between the time of the crash until the paramedics arrived?" Officer Brown asked.

"I don't know. I was unconscious after hitting my head on the dashboard." Quickly, I pointed to my dome. There was a three-inch cut from a shard of glass on my forehead, but they didn't know that, so I went with it. Truth was I was alert and very much conscious after the car finally landed on the roof. I even almost pissed on myself as one of Omar's goons approached our car to finish the job. He would have succeeded if it weren't for the fact that people were pulling over to offer help. Once he heard sirens, he disappeared.

"Do you know why someone would shoot at your fiancé's car?" Brown continued.

"No, I don't. Ken is well loved." I shook my head.

"Maybe he wasn't the one with enemies." Officer Kemp didn't bat an eyelash.

"What are you implying?" Now I was being defensive.

"A pretty little girl with a past meets the next Jordan and gets him to fall in love with her could warrant plenty of enemies, wouldn't you say?"

"Sounds logical to me," Brown added.

"Maybe one of your friends from the hood became jealous," Officer Kemp continued.

I was about to dog check his ass, but that was when Ken's mother came through the lobby, causing a scene.

"Is my baby okay?" She bum-rushed the front desk.

"I'm sorry. Who is your baby?" the receptionist asked.

"Ken Joseph Tucker."

"Excuse me, gentlemen. I need to speak with my mother-in-law." I stood without another word, then headed over to the small crowd of people behind her.

"May I go and see him please?" Mrs. Tucker begged the receptionist.

"Your son was in surgery all night, ma'am. As soon as he leaves the recovery area for his room in the intensive care unit, we will send you right up." The receptionist smiled. "Have a seat right there, and I'll come and get you as soon as Mr. Tucker is ready for visitors."

"Thank you." Mrs. Tucker and her family took a seat near the front desk, and I joined them.

"Excuse me, Mrs. Tucker. My name is Diamond. Ken is my boyfriend." I spoke softly. At first she looked at me like she couldn't care less, but then she smiled.

"How are you holding up, Diamond?"

"I'm okay, just a little shaken up." I took the seat across from her.

"This is your fault." A voice came from behind me. I looked up to see Ken's sister. I recognized her from a photo on his wall. Ken told me she was currently in the police academy. "My brother is a good boy. He's never done anything to anyone! You brought this trouble, didn't you?"

"Excuse me?" I was appalled.

"Bitch. My fucking brother is a multimillionaire. You better believe I do my research on everybody he comes in contact with."

"You got me twisted." I stood to prepare myself in case she started swinging.

"Diamond, my brother may not have known he was trying to wife a stripper, but I planned on telling him at Mama's birthday party."

"What does my past have to do with Ken loving me?" I challenged her.

"It has a lot to do with it when you're known for conning men for money," the sister whose name I couldn't remember barked back. I'm not going to lie. That one stung a lot. It was a grim reminder that I was who I was no matter how much I wanted to change.

"Diamond, I think it would be best for you to leave." Mrs. Tucker stood.

"I can't leave without Ken knowing I'm here." I felt so hurt. Ken was the first man I loved in a very long time. It killed me to know his family was denying me access in his time of need.

"Bullshit," the sister hollered.

"I'll make sure he knows." Mrs. Tucker took her seat and waited patiently for me to go.

With my head lowered, I nodded and walked away. I knew if Ken's family kicked me out of the hospital, they would have no problem kicking me out of his house. I had nowhere to go, but I did have his blank check in my purse from the other day. I could use it to buy myself a new life and new identity. By the time he got out of the hospital and realized what I had done, I'd be long gone, never to be seen or heard from again.

*Fuck Ken. Fuck California. Fuck Omar and Duck.* It was time for me to get the fuck out of dodge. I no longer gave a shit about who I owed. I was tired of looking over my shoulder. With Ken's money, I would be set for the rest of my life, no longer selling myself to men for money.

Anticipation and dollar signs had me dancing all the way home. Once I arrived, I began rummaging through Ken's belongings like a woman on a mission. I was sure he had a hidden stash somewhere around the house, and my greed wouldn't let me leave without it. However, when I heard the front door open, that was when I realized I had stayed a minute too long.

Quietly, I headed to the hallway and peered over the banister. Two gunmen were searching the downstairs. Their mouths were covered with blue bandanas, the same as the one the shooter wore yesterday. Therefore, I knew Omar had sent them. Slowly, I backed away and ran back into Ken's bedroom. Subsequent to grabbing my purse, I headed over to the balcony and used it to escape. The drop was only one story, so I jumped it with ease. As soon as my feet hit the dirt, I flew back toward the front of the condo like a track star.

After checking to ensure the coast was clear, I sprinted toward my car, then jumped in. Pulling off on two wheels, I was sure I left skid marks. "Hell yeah." I hit the steering wheel with excitement, completely finding it unbelievable that I had managed to get away with my life and the money.

I drove for nearly thirty minutes across town to the bank branch I used to frequent with Ken. Even though I wasn't on his account, I'd gone with him so many times that I had a rapport with a few of the staff members. After pulling into the parking lot, I killed the engine and pulled the folded check from my purse. Nervously, I stared at the paper before pulling out a pen and completing the document, signature and all. Forgery was something I learned back in school. My grades weren't too good, which meant I went home with a lot of papers for my mother to sign. When I got tired of punishments and ass whippings, I learned how to write her name perfectly.

Over time, I learned other people's as well. Ken's signature was one of them, and it was relatively easy. It was the first letter in his first and last names, then one squiggly line following each one.

"Now you ain't trying to ditch me without repaying your debt, are you?" Duck's voice startled me. He'd been lying on the floor for the entire ride.

"Shit," I hollered before looking into the rearview mirror. Duck had a gun pointed at the back of my seat. "I wasn't trying to ditch no one. I got your money right here." I waved the check. "I just need to go in there and cash it."

"I'm going with you."

"You can't. I've never gone in there with anyone besides Ken. If I show up with you and a large check payable to me, they will know something is up." I couldn't believe I'd been so close to walking away scot-free. Duck showing up wasn't going to stop my plan though.

"Fine. I'll wait here, but don't take long." He nodded for me to get out, and I did.

With my head held high and strutting like a peacock, I swung the door open to First National and approached the teller.

"Hey, Diamond, where's the big guy?" Lula, my favorite of all the tellers, asked.

"I don't know if you heard, but we had a pretty bad accident yesterday." I pointed to my head. "Ken had to have surgery. He'll be down for a while."

"Oh, my goodness. I'm sorry to hear that. This is news to me." Lula shook her head. "Is he all right though?"

"It's pretty bad." I nodded before producing the check and laying it on the counter. "His family has come up from Alabama and taken over. They even had the nerve to kick me out of the hospital. Can you believe that?"

"I know how it is. The same thing happened to my sister when her boyfriend of fifteen years died from cancer. The family put her out of his house and told her she couldn't help plan the funeral and to not even show up at the services." Lula paused before picking up the check, then fixating on it.

"Ken didn't want me to be without while he went through this fight for his life, so he gave me a little something to hold me down because he knew his mother wouldn't." I tried to look depressed for dramatic effect.

"Diamond, this is a lot of money. I have to speak with my manager first. Have a seat and I'll be back, okay?" Lula smiled and backed away. Before I could even get comfortable on the sofa, she was back. "He said it's a go. Give me time to get it ready, and then you'll be good to go."

"Really?" I caught myself and cleaned it up. "Good, I thought I would be in here all day." Feeling a little more confident, I grabbed a magazine, sat back, and crossed my legs.

During the entire forty minutes I waited, I couldn't stop the smile from displaying on my face. The thought of being a millionaire had me tickled pink. I was so caught up in my thoughts that I was oblivious to those around me. Life was about to change, and I couldn't wait.

"She's right there," I heard Lula say, and then I looked up to see who she was talking to.

"Diamond Herrington, please stand. You're under arrest for grand larceny."

# Chapter Twenty-eight

## *Jasmine*

"Jasmine James, on the charge of possession, how do you plead?" the white heavyset judge asked me the next day.

I pondered my answer for a quick second. *That shit was not mine. Hell, I didn't even know it was in my purse, Your Honor.* I thought about saying what was on my mind. Instead, one word tumbled out. "Guilty."

"Typically, in a case like this, I recommend twelve to eighteen months of jail time or a mandatory six-month stay at a drug rehabilitation center for addicts in need of recovery." He removed his glasses, and I swallowed hard because I couldn't do either jail or rehab.

"However, Mrs. James, because this is your first offense and your urine samples from the lab were clean," Judge J.D. Waters spoke through the closed-circuit television, "I'm letting you off with a fine of fifteen hundred dollars and a warning to never be caught in this situation again, understood?"

"Yes, sir, Your Honor sir," I practically shouted.

"We will enter your plea of guilty and your release agreement into the system. Your court fees are an additional two hundred dollars. Your release will be granted once payment in full for bail and court fees have been obtained. Court adjourned."

I was so happy that I could've kissed him. In a matter of an hour, I was a free woman. My mother still had not answered her phone, and I was worried to death. Lizzie handed me my purse and cell phone, which Sheriff Johnson had confiscated yesterday. The minute I powered my cell up, text messages and voicemails came left and right. The first few messages were from Stacey, so I deleted them ASAP. The last few were from my mom. The hairs on the back of my neck stood up.

"Hey, baby, it's Mama." She sniffed. "Call me when you get this. I'm at Michigan Valley Hospital." She sniffed again. "Just get here when you can, baby, okay? My phone is going to die. Just get here."

My heart raced. I knew something wasn't right. I called a cab, and within minutes I was on my way to the hospital. I tried my mom again but there was no answer. Next I called King.

"You out?"

"Surprised?" I snapped.

"So what's up? What do you want?" he asked with a little irritation.

"Have you spoken to my mother? She called from Michigan Valley, crying and upset."

"She was blowing my phone up like crazy yesterday. I didn't answer because I was busy, and I thought it was about you being locked up," he admitted.

"I hope everything is okay with Jordan." Panic was evident in my voice.

"That little nigga is all right. Stop worrying and call me back later. They're waiting for me to shoot this next part." King hung up before I had the chance to say bye, or anything else for that matter.

Placing my phone back inside my purse, I closed my eyes and prayed that everything was okay. Maybe Jordan had a cold or something. My mother was more overprotective than I was when it came to him. She probably noticed something small like a runny nose or slight cough and took him to see a doctor.


"Thirty-five dollars." The Arab driver pulled in front of the hospital. I pulled out two twenties, slid them through the mini-door, and told him to keep the change. I walked through the revolving door of the hospital, then marched right up to the receptionist.

"Hi, I'm looking for Jordan James or Wanda Foster." I gave both names because I wasn't sure if the patient was Jordan or my mother. The dark-skinned clerk with the finger-waved eighties hairdo typed vigorously. I scanned the waiting area in search of my mother while I waited.

"Oh." She looked up in horror. "Give me one second. I'll have someone come and get you." She lifted a red painted index finger, indicating one moment.

I rolled my eyes and sighed loudly. The anxiety was about to kill me, but I didn't want to take my frustrations out on her, so I walked away. I was pacing back and forth for approximately ten minutes before a guy in green scrubs and a white lab coat approached me.

"Please, ma'am, follow me," he said, then turned away. I was hot on his trail. I thought it was odd that he didn't greet me like a normal doctor would, but I was just trying to get to my family, so I didn't say anything. We stepped onto the elevator in silence. I watched as he pressed the button for the ground floor, causing me to raise an eyebrow. Never had I been taken to the basement of a hospital. Thus, I wondered just what in the hell was going on.

"What's down here?"

"Your mother is down here waiting for you," he replied without looking at me. The elevator buzzed, and then we stepped off. "Right this way." The man nodded and we turned left. I held my breath as we walked past an office door, an employee break room, and a large door marked TRASH. Just as I was about to ask him again where we were going, my mother ran over to me with her arms wide open.

# Chapter Twenty-nine

## *Lyric*

After leaving the police station yesterday, it seemed that my streak of bad luck had returned. Not only did Ken want all the money I'd already spent, but then Damien received a call on the way home advising us that his movie didn't get the proper financing it needed. Therefore, they were cancelling production. Furthermore, after my mug shot for shoplifting made its way online, the media had a field day with the story. Before I knew it, my phone was blowing up with clients either demanding an explanation or wanting to drop me all together. To top things off, I'd missed my flight to Puerto Rico.

"Do you want something to eat? I'm taking the kids out for burgers." Damien poked his head inside the bedroom. With all the shades pulled, the room was completely black. I was buried beneath the covers with the pillow over my face.

"We don't have money for burgers," I reminded him.

"Lyric, we'll figure this out."

"We need to sell the house before the bank takes it." My mind was on autopilot. All I could think of was where to go from here. "I'm calling the car company, too. They can have their shit as well."

"Let's not be so extreme, baby." Damien stepped farther into the room.

"I'm not being extreme. I'm being realistic." I sat up. "Fuck it all. Fuck everybody. I'm tired of pretending. I'm tired of it all," I rambled.

"Lyric, you're not the losing kind. Don't let one battle bring you down." Damien rested a hand on my shoulder.

"I'm tired of fighting a battle I'm never going to win."

"Daddy, come on," Leslie called from the hallway.

"Let's finish this when I get back, okay?" Damien kissed my lips softly, and I felt a tear slide down my check.

"Love you, Damien. Tell the kids I love them too," I blurted out as he closed the bedroom door.

My husband was right. I wasn't a loser. Lyric Nicole Robertson always had a game plan for my family, even if it meant sacrificing myself in the process. "The insurance policy." I sprang from the bed, went to the safe in the closet, and retrieved the folder marked "Important." It contained birth certificates, social security cards, and our insurance policies. Quickly, I scanned through the pages and smiled. If something were to happen to me, my children would receive $1 million each to be dispensed in $200,000 increments at ages 18, 21, 25, 30, and 35. Damien would receive his million in increments every two years, provided he passed random drug tests set up by my attorney. The policy was something I put in place after Damien's first drug debacle. Now I was happy that I had always managed to make my annual payments.

Staring at the document and knowing what I was about to do, reality hit me hard. Nonetheless, I was determined not to change my mind. Heading over to the bathroom, I grabbed some pain meds from the time I broke my leg last year at Leslie's skating party. The bottle was nearly full of Percocet when I tipped it back and began swallowing. Reaching for the glass on the counter I gargled with in the morning, I filled it with water and continued digesting the pills.

Before they kicked in, I took one last look in the mirror, then went to lie down in bed. I didn't want to write any letters because I didn't want my children to remember me by final words. I didn't want to make any calls either because I didn't want anyone to stop me. All I wanted was peace and to be free of my burdens.

Closing my eyes, I calmly breathed in and out, trying to relax my mind. Rather quickly, I began to hallucinate, and then my breathing became slower and shorter. It felt as if someone were holding a pillow over my face, and I began to burn up. I tried to raise my arms to lift the imaginary pillow, but my body wouldn't move. Blinking hastily, I tried hard to focus. No longer did I like this feeling. I needed to grab the phone and call for help.

"I don't want to die," I mumbled as my heart started racing. "Help me!"

"Lyric, what did you do? Oh, my God! Leslie, call 911." I could hear Damien and my children screaming, but it was too late. Within an instant, everything went dark. It was lights out for Lyric Nicole Richardson. The curtain had finally closed on my life.

# Chapter Thirty

## *Jasmine*

"Hey, Mama, are you okay?" I asked because she was visibly upset and shaken by something.

"Oh, baby, my beautiful baby." She dabbed at her eyes with a crumbled piece of Kleenex.

"What's wrong, Mama? Where's Jordan?" I strained my neck to look over her shoulder.

"Come and sit down with me, baby." She pulled me toward a set of chairs leaning against the stale yellow wall.

"Mama, you're really scaring me right now. Where is my baby?" I had started to cry, and I hadn't even received any news yet. I could tell by the feeling deep in the pit of my stomach that something was wrong, just like the day Jordan was born. My mother patted my back, then looked up toward the heavens.

"Baby, Jordan has gone on to be with the Lord in His kingdom," she said, but it didn't quite register with me.

"Jordan went where? And to be with who?" I questioned.

"Jasmine, Jordan has gone on to glory, baby. Mama wants you to be strong, okay?" She held me as I collapsed into her arms.

"Are you saying my child is dead?" I screamed, and she nodded with a tearstained face. "When did this happen, Mama?" Closing my eyes, I pulled on my hair.

"Yesterday afternoon I went to wake him up from his nap for lunch, and he was gone. The Lord took him in his sleep, Jasmine. I'm so sorry, baby. I'm so very sorry." My mother sniffled. "I tried to reach you and King, but I couldn't get either of you."

"You've been here since yesterday?" I asked as guilt set in. I should've been with my son before he was called to heaven. I should've been the one here at the hospital all day. But instead I was locked up behind King's bullshit. The more I thought about things, the angrier I was becoming.

"Yes, baby, I've been sitting right here." She paused to blow her nose. "I just couldn't leave him, Jasmine. I couldn't leave him all alone in there by himself." She cried and pointed to the window behind us. "Jordan was such a good boy. I just wish his dad had given him a chance."

The words that she spoke made my blood boil because it was absolutely true. Instead of loving and caring for our son, King treated him like he was nothing and didn't matter. "Mama, what am I going to do now? My only reason for breathing was Jordan, and God took him from me."

I was mad at the world, including the Lord Himself. Dammit! I was a good person. I did nice things for people and spoke kind words to everyone. So why would this happen to me? "Mama, you know the Lord, right?" My nostrils flared. "Ask Him why He did this. Didn't God know that I needed my son in order to survive? Without Jordan, I'm dead. You might as well bury me too," I declared.

"Jasmine, you stop that, you hear me? God will never put more on us than we can bear. Do you understand that, baby?" She rubbed my back as I released all of my pain, tears, and frustration. "The Lord loaned Jordan to us for four beautiful years, but he was ready for His son to come home. You are a great mom, and you always will be a wonderful person. This had nothing to do with you. Jordan's life, no matter how short, was predestined, and it was God's will for him to go home."

My mother was right, but I couldn't help the way I was feeling. I just prayed that God would understand. I laid my head down on my mother's lap as she rocked me like an infant. So many thoughts ran through my mind that my head began to throb. I was a ball of emotions. I couldn't stop the pain. I felt hurt, angry, upset, betrayed, and lonely.

"Jasmine, do you want to see Jordan before the funeral home comes to pick him up?"

"No, Mama. You go ahead. I can't." Shaking my head, I stood up from the blue plastic chair and went to get some air. On my way outside, I called King.

"Yeah," he answered on the third ring.

"King, it's Jordan. He died, baby. Our son is gone." I cried hysterically.

"Stop, I'm on the phone. You play too much," he said to some girl giggling in the background. "Jasmine, you said what?" King asked, and I rolled my eyes.

"I said our son is fucking dead!" I snapped, causing several people to stop and stare at me.

"Damn, I'm sorry to hear that. Are you okay? Do you need anything?" he asked like a friend of the family would. Didn't he realize Jordan was his son too?

"Yes, King, I do need something. I need you to be here! You've never been there for your son during his whole life. Can't you at least make him a priority now that he's gone?" I screamed into the receiver.

"Chill the fuck out with that yelling. I'll be home tomorrow, and I'll see you then," he snarled.

"So you telling me a motherfucking music video is more important than your son?" I was fuming.

"I didn't say all of that, Jasmine, but this is how I get paid. Somebody has to make the money to pay for his funeral, right?" he barked, and I stood speechless. "That's what I thought! Like I said, I'll be home tomorrow."

# Chapter Thirty-one

## *Tionne*

As Zuri slept peacefully in my hotel bed, I had quietly grabbed the keys to my car, which hadn't been repossessed yet, and exited the room. We had planned to go over to her house and collect her things later this evening, but I wasn't stupid. We needed protection, and I knew just where to get it. Dallas and I both had our license to carry concealed weapons as well as an arsenal of firearms, so I headed home, a place I never thought I would see again.

Within twenty minutes, I was pulling up to the gate and punching in the code. I half expected that Dallas had changed it as well as the locks, but like magic, the doors parted like the Red Sea. Pulling into the large driveway, I noticed that Dallas's car was gone, and I exhaled. His not being here really made my task a lot easier. It would also give me a chance to grab some of the shit I should've grabbed when I initially left before I found out I was broke. Truthfully, I was a tad homesick, and the sight of my mansion made me miss everything about my old life. It was nice to live carefree even if I had to deal with a few bitches here and there. Zuri's situation made me realize that I didn't have it that bad. *Maybe Dallas and I can work it out and seek counseling?* I thought before remembering the dreaded call from the doctor's office.

What if it was AIDS? The conversation I remembered having not long ago with Zuri played in my head.

Shaking off my thoughts, I stepped from the whip and proceeded to the door. After sliding my key into the lock, I prayed it worked, which it did. Once inside the house, I flew to the alarm panel. Surprisingly, it wasn't armed. "Just like Dallas to be so careless," I mumbled before turning to face the mess of clothes, pizza boxes, and other shit thrown all over the place. "Some things never change." Dallas had really been partying in my absence. Shay, the maid, was going to go ape shit when she saw this place. It would take her two days to get it right and get the smell of feet and old food out of the furniture.

Remembering the task at hand, I hurriedly ran through the house, searching for the key to the gun cabinet that was sitting along the wall of our family room. It wasn't in the kitchen drawer or the desk drawer in Dallas's office. That was when I remembered he had moved the key up to our bedroom, where he kept it in the nightstand. Taking them two by two, I made it up the stairs to our room door, which was closed. Without hesitation, I barged right in. What I saw next had my mouth dragging the floor. Dallas was naked in bed with not one but two people, and both of them were men.

When the shock of what I was seeing finally wore off, I removed my cell phone and did the first thing that came to mind. I started snapping pictures like the paparazzi. Realizing photos of Dallas spooning a man and holding his waist while another sandwiched him were priceless, I was sure to get one from every angle. One of the men began to stir. I almost pissed myself when I saw Gangsta Goonie, a notorious West Coast rapper known for being a bully in the industry.

"What the fuck." He began tapping the others to wake them up.

Thinking fast, I grabbed the key from the nightstand and flew downstairs to the gun cabinet.

No sooner than I had two Smith & Wessons in hand did Dallas bring his gay ass down the stairs. "Tionne, what are you doing?" he asked like I hadn't just caught him in bed with two dudes.

"Securing my future," I snapped.

"What?"

"Yeah, buddy, you and your friends are going to pay big time for the fun you had last night. I want twenty million dollars in my account by tomorrow, or these pictures get leaked."

"You wouldn't dare."

Dallas tried to come for me, but I let off a warning shot to back him up. He knew from our time at the gun range that my precision with a weapon was deadly. Therefore, he dared not make a move.

"The tabloids would probably pay twice as much. As a matter of fact, I might just call them." I slowly backed toward the door.

"All right, you got it. Twenty million in your account tomorrow." Dallas had his hands raised in surrender.

"I want one mil from big man too." I nodded to Goonie, who was at the top of the stairs. He wasn't worth nearly as much as my husband. One million was probably all he had.

"Whatever you want, it's yours." Dallas gritted his teeth. "Just give me the phone."

"You'll get the phone when I get the money." Tucking one of the guns under my arm, I unlocked the door, then hauled ass to my car.

# Chapter Thirty-two

## *Zuri*

After awaking from my power nap, I had to hit the ground running in Tionne's absence. As much as I wanted to wait for her, I knew my window of opportunity was small. Jason would be home in less than three hours. Therefore, I had to get going. "Shit," I said, suddenly remembering that I didn't have a car. Thinking fast, I grabbed my phone and dialed Lyric.

"Hey, this is your girl Lyric. I'm unavailable at the moment. Leave me a message, and I'll call you back as soon as I'm able. Have a great day and remember that I love you."

"Hey, Lyric, it's me. I was calling you for a ride. If you're free, call me back. Love you too, girl." I ended the call with a smile. My girl Lyric was a firm believer in saying she loved you at the end of every call to all her family and friends. I used to think it was strange before she explained her reasoning.

"Girl, people don't last forever, so you never want to miss the opportunity to say I love you," Lyric would always say. She was the reason I now said it all the time as well.

After calling Tionne twice, I finally gave up and grabbed the hotel phone to dial out.

"Front desk. This is Sarah."

"Hi, Sarah, can you please call a metro car for me?" I said while slipping into my shoes.

"There is actually one out front already."

"Good. I'll be right down." Grabbing my purse from the desktop, I ended the call and flew out the door.

The entire ride home had me nervous and sick to my stomach. There were so many questions weighing heavy on my mind that it was becoming hard to think. I knew I was making the best decision for myself and Jelly, but somehow I didn't feel right about it. I felt like a criminal sneaking into my own home, stealing my belongings, and ultimately kidnapping my daughter. Speaking of Jelly, I wondered how my actions would affect her. It wasn't fair to keep her away from Jason, but right now I had to do what I had to do.

"Missus, I said we're here." The driver of the metro car sat idling in my driveway. "Would you like me to wait for you?"

"Um, no. I'm good," I said before handing him a $20 tip. The bill for the service had been added to the account we already had with them.

"Have a good day," the driver said as I stepped out and closed the door.

Just as I approached the door, it popped open, and I jumped. "Hi, Mrs. Armstrong. I wasn't expecting you back for a few days." Helen, the nanny, greeted me with a smile. She was holding Jelly, who immediately reached for me when she saw me.

"There was a change of plans." I took hold of my daughter and kissed her soft lips. "Where is Sylvia?"

"She just left for her daily walk around the neighborhood." Helen closed the door and followed me into the house.

"I need you to take Jelly upstairs to get dressed. Then go to the MKX in the garage and strap her in. Stay with her in the car until I come out there, okay?" I kissed Jelly once more before handing her over.

"Yes, ma'am." Helen didn't ask any questions, which I liked about her. She simply nodded her understanding, then flew up the stairs. I raced up behind her as fast as I could. My side was still hurting, but the adrenaline racing through my veins had me going.

The minute I hit the top step, I entered my bedroom and went over to my side of the bed. After lifting the sheets, I ran my hand along the edges until I found the slit I'd cut years ago. It was one of my hiding spots that housed a few stacks of money. Hastily, I retrieved what was in there and tossed them on top of the bed. Next, I went over to the closet and grabbed two Dooney & Bourke duffle bags. One of them was empty, and the other served as another one of my hiding spots. It too was filled partially with money. One thing I learned a long time ago was to not trust the bank with all of your dough. After tossing the money on the bed into the bag, I took both bags into my daughter's room. Helen had just finished putting her shoes on. Jelly was trying to eat them while sitting in her car seat.

"Helen, can you take her stroller downstairs for me?"

"Yes, ma'am."

"Thank you." I nodded before grabbing Jelly's diapers, wipes, toys, and a few articles of clothing, then tossing them in the empty bag. Glancing down at my watch, I saw I was making good time, or so I thought until I heard the front door open and Helen address Jason. "Fuck." Right at this moment, I could've passed out, but I knew if I stopped now, I'd be here forever.

"Zuri." The sound of Jason calling my name locked my bowels up instantly.

Without responding, I zipped up the bag and grabbed the other one and Jelly's car seat in one swift motion.

"Didn't you hear me calling you?"

"No, I didn't," I replied before turning to face him.

"When did you come back? What happened?" Jason walked into the room, then stood behind me.

"Tionne left her passport, and Lyric never showed up." Finally, I turned around slowly.

"Where are you going?" He looked down at the bags and the car seat.

"Well, I thought I would take Jelly to spend a few nights with Aunt T," I lied with a straight face. "She's been having a tough time lately and was really looking forward to our girl time."

"You must think I'm stupid." Jason's jaw muscle clenched. "I saw you on the surveillance tape packing your money." With a closed fist, my husband rocked my face, sending me stumbling backward. I'd completely forgotten about the nearly invisible cameras we had throughout our home.

"Are you leaving me?"

"Yes, Jason. I'm leaving and I'm never coming back. Fuck you and your money." I tried to barge past him, but he caught me with a left hook and then a right. Losing my balance, I dropped both of the duffle bags and Jelly's car seat to the floor, then hit the floor myself. Just as Jason lifted his right foot to kick me, I crawled over to his left leg and bit him so hard that I was sure I drew blood.

"Bitch." He kneeled down to check out his leg. When he did, I snatched the lamp off the table near the rocking chair where I sometimes read to Jelly, and I broke it across his face.

By now, Jason was seething, but I'd bought enough time to stand and grab Jelly and one duffle bag and make it into the hallway.

"You will never leave me, Zuri!" Jason yelled from the bedroom.

"Fuck you. I'm done." Although my body was weak, my feet kept moving toward the staircase.

"The only way you're leaving is in a body bag. Do you hear me?" Jason was now in the hallway behind me. "Do you hear me? In a fucking body bag." He flew toward me just as I looked back. The fury in his eyes had replaced the brown pupils I once knew to be kind and gentle. My husband was possessed and completely unaware of what he was doing when he tackled me at the exact time that I approached the edge of the stairs.

"No!" Sylvia screamed from the foyer.

I felt myself falling and watched in slow motion as she and Helen covered their eyes in horror when Jelly and I both went tumbling down the spiral staircase with force. Desperately, I tried to protect my daughter as she screamed for dear life, but there was nothing I could do. The sound of my head hitting the hard tile was loud enough for me to know that I was bleeding and hurt pretty bad. Finally, my body reached the foyer. By then, I couldn't see or hear anything. I couldn't move either.

# Chapter Thirty-three

## *Jasmine*

Just as I was about to call King back, my cell phone vibrated. It was Stacey. "Bitch, don't ever call my mother-fucking phone again in life," I warned.

"What did I do to you?" she asked. "I should be the one mad. I haven't heard from you in two weeks."

"And you won't ever hear from me again once we end this phone call with your phony ass."

"Phony? Please. I'm the realest bitch you know," Stacey stated matter-of-factly.

"You were the realest bitch I knew up until you let your stank-ass sister fuck my husband and make two babies." I bit down on my bottom lip until I tasted blood.

"Wait a minute, what?" She played dumb.

"Don't act like you didn't know, Stacey. Just woman up and tell the truth." I hailed one of the cabs lingering by the curb. I needed to leave this hospital and fast.

"Look," she sighed, "I knew they fucked once way back in the day before he got locked up, but I swear I didn't know they started messing around again."

"Fuck messing around. I could get over that shit," I told her. "That bitch had his babies, and that's not cool, Stacey. When I see your sister, I'm going to fuck her up on sight. I would advise you not to jump in if you don't want to get fucked up too," I warned her, and I meant it. When I faced off with Tracey, I wanted it to be one-on-one, but if Stacey jumped in, I had something for her ass too.

"Are you sure those are his kids? They don't even look like him." She was right. They didn't look like him. They looked dead like their mom, but I knew it had to be true if King was claiming them.

"King, Prince, and Princess. Do you get it now?" I said, pulling the phone away from my face to give the cab driver my address. "You ain't got shit to say about that, huh?" I put the phone back up to my ear.

"Jasmine, I'm so very sorry," was the best she could come up with.

"Well, save your sorry. I've had more than my share of 'sorry' for this lifetime." I wiped at the silent tears slipping down my face. "I'm sorry that you're a snake. I'm sorry that your sister is a slut. I'm sorry that my husband ain't shit, and I'm fucking sorry that my son had to die."

"Die? Jasmine, what do you mean he had to die?" She was confused.

"Die, as in dead. My son didn't fucking wake up yesterday afternoon." I got choked up just saying the words.

"Oh, my God. Where are you? I'm on my way."

"Please stay the fuck away from me," I urged and ended the call. I wasn't in the best mental space at the moment. Therefore, I needed time to myself. I hoped she would respect my wishes and leave me alone, especially for her own safety. With all the pent-up anger and rage in my heart, I was liable to do anything.

Thirty minutes later, the cab pulled up to my gate. I paid the driver, punched the code in, and walked up my circular driveway in silence. Taking in the scenery acre by acre, I surveyed the house that I used to love so much. I had only been gone for a day, but everything looked different, sort of foreign. Placing my key into the front door, I paused, took a deep breath, then turned the key. It felt out of place to be there, and I was extremely uneasy. I ran up the stairs into my bedroom. Rummaging through my belongings like a madwoman, I raced around the room packing all of my sentimental items. I packed a few pieces of clothing, grabbed two pairs of shoes, and all of my and Jordan's personal documents. Yesterday, I had a plan to take it all. Today, I just wanted to leave with what I had come here with.

I pulled my wedding ring and band off, placing them both on King's nightstand. I headed downstairs to the garage but stopped in my tracks as the large oil painting of me holding Jordan when he was a baby caught my attention. We had commissioned it when he was 2 months old, and I adored it. The inscription on the bottom of the gold frame made me cry as I read it aloud.

*There is an enduring tenderness in the love of a mother to a son that transcends all other affections of the heart.*
*—Washington Irving*

Wiping my eyes, I reached up and removed it from the wall. This would be my way of taking a piece of my son with me.

Just as I loaded up the Navigator, my cell phone rang. "Didn't I tell you to leave me the hell alone?" I snapped because I figured it was Stacey.

"Where did you go, baby?" My mama asked, full of concern.

"Oh, Mama, I'm sorry. I thought you were Stacey. I had to come home and get a few things. I'm sorry, but I couldn't stay at that hospital," I apologized.

"I understand, baby. Well, did you get a hold of King?"

"Yes, ma'am, I did, but you already know how that went." I smacked my lips as my line beeped. "Mama, I'm on my way to your house. I'll see you in a few minutes, okay?" I said and clicked over. "Hello?" I waited for someone to respond. I glanced at the caller ID. It was a private call. "Who the fuck is this?" I got into the driver's seat, then pulled away from the garage.

"It's the bitch who's fucking your man," the caller said.

"So this must be Tracey's stank ass or one of his other baby mamas," I cut into her, and she smacked her lips.

"So how does it feel to know you got played? I been fucking him the whole time y'all been together," she boasted proudly.

"You and every bitch he comes in contact with." I laughed but she didn't.

"Anyway, Jasmine, I was just calling to let you know that your man been with me the last two days. He ain't at no damn video shoot. His ass been lying next to me like he always does when he tells you he's out of town."

"If y'all been playing house and he's been lying about being out of town, why you calling to let me know now?" I parked the truck and waited for her answer.

"Because King is finally going to leave you."

"Good, because I'm sick of him anyway. Congrats and best wishes," I said, reaching to tap the end button on my phone.

"He was going to leave you after you had Jordan," Tracey blurted out. "But then his publicist Danielle told him it wouldn't look good for his image to leave the mother of his special-needs son."

"Keep my son's name out of your mouth," I advised.

"Nevertheless, now that your son is gone, me, him, and our kids can finally be a family."

"Tracey, don't mention my son again if you want to live to see another day." I would kill this ho in a heartbeat, and that was a promise.

"What are you going to do?" she tried me.

"Tracey, don't test my gangster!"

"Anyway, Jasmine, have a nice life. You ain't got no son, no husband, and you won't have no money because I bet your dumb ass signed a prenuptial agreement." She laughed. "You might as well go kill yourself."

"Actually, that's not a bad idea," I agreed, causing her to fall silent. She was wrong about me signing a prenup. Actually, I was entitled to half of everything King owned. However, she was right about me being alone. Without Jordan, neither the money nor the possessions meant a thing to me. What did I have to look forward to in the morning? Nothing. So why not off myself? Hell, if I was going out, why not take King and his mistress with me? I laughed hysterically, making Tracey uneasy.

I hung up on Tracey, who I was sure was freaking out right now, and I called the cell phone company.

"Hello, Mrs. James. What can I do for you today?" Stephanie, my personal Sprint representative, asked. She was assigned to us when King became famous. She handled our account personally and kept our records confidential from the public and other Sprint employees.

"Hey, Stephanie, King lost his phone. We need to either find it or have it turned off. We think it's still here at the hotel in the room we're staying in, so I wanted you to check the GPS tracking device for me." I lied because I needed to know where King was.

"Mrs. James, you're right. The phone is still at the Dell Hotel. I show that it was last active about thirty minutes ago," she confirmed.

"Thanks, Stephanie. Have a good one." I smiled and ended the call. His ass was just up the street from our house. How convenient.

I ran back into the house and into King's study. I used the small key on the key ring to unlock the bottom drawer of his desk. Staring back at me was a nickel-plated 9 mm. Without hesitation, I reached for it. After checking for bullets, I dropped it into my purse and hopped back into my SUV, leaving my front door wide open. I felt myself losing it and tried to reason with my alter ego all the way over to the hotel. Unfortunately, she wasn't having it. This was her breaking point, and I could do nothing to stop her.

Pulling into the parking lot on two wheels, I put the SUV in park, and hopped out right at the door.

"Thank you for visiting the Dell. How can I help you?" a young African American girl asked with a bucktooth smile as large as Texas.

"Hey, Shanika." I looked at her gold name tag. "My husband, King James, is here, and I need to know in what room." I wasn't trying to pretend anymore, so I didn't have to make up a story with her.

"Um, I can't give out that information, ma'am."

"Will this help you?" I placed $500 on top of the black countertop.

Nervously, she looked from side to side before sliding the money toward her. Then she tapped on the keyboard and looked up at me.

"Room 616," she whispered.

# Chapter Thirty-four

## *Jasmine*

I tried to talk myself out of what I was about to do, but it wasn't working. My mind was on overload with everything on my plate. I stepped from the elevator and pulled the gun from my purse. A couple passed me in the hallway and gasped, but I no longer cared or had control over my actions. It was at this moment that I realized how people snapped and claimed temporary insanity. I was going to do what I came here for, and it didn't matter to me if I left in handcuffs or a body bag.

I banged on the door.

"Who is that knocking like the police?" I heard King say.

"You go ahead and shower. I'll get it, baby," Tracey called back to him as she swung the door open. "What the hell?"

"Room service, bitch." I pushed my nickel-plated nine up against her chest and forced my way into the hotel suite.

"It's like that, Jasmine?" she asked while trying to cover her butt-naked ass.

"Yeah, bitch, it's definitely like that." I pulled the trigger without a second thought. Tracey stumbled a few times, finally falling backward and shattering the glass coffee table. I walked up and stood over her. "See what fucking my husband got you?" I asked. "Now you tell me if it was worth it."

"Please," she barely whispered as she gurgled blood around in her throat.

"Please what? Speak up. I can't hear you," I taunted. "You thought you were big shit over the phone, didn't you?" I shot her trifling ass again as an afterthought.

King flew from the bathroom with a white towel wrapped around his waist. "Jasmine, what the fuck?" was all he said before I aimed the gun at him.

"I was the last person you expected to see today, right?" I asked. "Your lying ass was here laid up this whole time with this bitch. You were less than twenty minutes away from the hospital and couldn't come and say goodbye to your son?" I wagged my finger. "Bad move!"

"Jasmine, I was working," he said, continuing to lie.

"You call this work? Yeah, right. This is some video set." I faked a smile, and he shifted nervously. "You must've been making a porno instead of a music video." I laughed wickedly as I scanned the room with disgust. There were several shopping bags, liquor bottles, and condom wrappers scattered throughout the room. These two scum buckets were up in here fucking and living it up while I was in jail and my son was lying in the morgue.

"Jasmine, let me explain," he pleaded like a bitch.

"There is nothing to explain, King. The writing is on the wall, and you gave it to me straight the other night, remember?" I stepped over Tracey's dead body and walked toward my husband.

"Put the gun down," King begged.

"Or what? What are you going to do, hit me?" I dared him to make a move. The minute he moved an inch, I was busting a cap in his ass.

"Jasmine, you don't really want to hurt me, do you?" he asked like this was a game.

"Why not? You've hurt me plenty of times. Over and over, you continued to treat me like the shit on the bottom of your shoe." I stepped forward, which made King so nervous that he let go of the towel, raising both his hands in the air. The sight of his shriveled-up dick made me sick to my stomach. I aimed right between his legs and blew his dick off, balls and all.

"Oh, shit." King dropped down to his knees, rolling around on the floor in pain.

"Guess you won't be making any more babies, huh?" I went and bent down beside him. "That shit hurts like hell, doesn't it?"

"Why you doing this?"

"Because I'm sick and tired of your bullshit. I've come to the end of my rope, and you've come to the end of the road." I stood right over him with my gun pointed at his head.

"What you saying, Jas?" King looked scared shitless.

"I'm saying that you better make peace because you're about to meet your Maker." I pressed the gun to the middle of his forehead.

"You going to hell, Jasmine. Do you hear me?" King cried.

"Then I guess I'll 'see you at the crossroads . . . so you won't be lonely.'" I sang the Bone Thugs-N-Harmony lyric and squeezed the trigger.

I couldn't explain it, but I wasn't scared or remorseful for what I'd just done. In fact, I felt vindicated and relieved. My nerves were calm, my heart rate was steady, and I felt like a new woman. I picked up the hotel's cordless phone and walked into the bathroom. Staring at my reflection in the mirror, I no longer saw a woman dying to be loved and appreciated. No, the reflection staring back at me was that of a warrior, a fighter, an independent woman with no more tears! Dialing 911, I smiled at the new me.

"911, what's the emergency?" a chipper operator answered the call.

"I would like to report a double homicide."

"Excuse me, but did you say you're calling to report a double homicide?" the operator asked.

"Yes! Two people are dead," I said calmly.

"What's your location?"

"I'm at the Dell Hotel in room 616," I answered.

"Okay, stay calm. Police and emergency medical units have been dispatched. Help is on the way." The operator sounded alarmed. "Are you in any danger?"

"No. Not anymore," I replied, feeling the safest I'd felt in a very long time.

"Is the assailant still on the premises? Is he or she nearby?"

"Yes, she's here. As a matter of fact, she's so close I can touch her," I said while placing the palm of my hand against the mirror.

"I'm going to stay on the phone with you until help arrives," the operator conveyed.

"Help better get here fast before there's one more body added to the number." Dropping the phone into the sink, I placed the gun to my head, prepared to take what was left of my existence.

Before I could pull the trigger, I was bum-rushed by two male police officers. "Put the gun down," one of them yelled as the other one snatched it from my hand.

Once again, I was placed under arrest and handcuffed. I guessed someone had heard the gunshots or the couple in the hallway must've called the police because they showed up extremely fast.

"Aww shit! That's KJ, the famous rapper from Independent Records," the young black cop stated for the other cop to hear.

"Damn, she blew his dick off," the young white cop confirmed after getting a closer look. He sat me down on the bed, then pulled out his cell phone to take a few pictures of the bloody crime scene.

"I'm about to get paid." He laughed along with his partner.

"Yeah, I heard *Sloppy Gossip* magazine pays top-notch for shit like this." The black guy pulled out his phone as well and followed suit. This foolishness went on for another twenty minutes as I sat and waited to be taken to jail.

"Damn, shorty, what these people do to you?" the black cop asked.

"More than you can imagine," was my reply.

"It must've been pretty messed up for you to go this far. You don't even look like the type to do some stuff like this. This right here is just cold-blooded," the white cop added as he helped me stand from the bed and walked me toward the door.

"You do realize that you just flushed all your fame and fortune down the drain, right?" the black officer asked.

I stopped dead in my tracks and looked back at Tracey then at King for the last time. "I guess when a woman's fed up, fame and fortune don't mean shit!"

## *The End*